BAD
WOLF

❦

A CAT MCKENZIE NOVEL

USA TODAY BESTSELLING AUTHOR

LAUREN DAWES

BAD
WOLF

A CAT MCKENZIE NOVEL

Bad Wolf
(A Snarky Paranormal Detective Story)
Cat McKenzie Series #4

Print: 978-1-922353-34-4

Cover design by Deranged Doctor Designs
Edited by Swish Design & Editing
Proofread by Swish Design & Editing

For Leila

1

"It's a dildo," my best friend said slowly, turning the rectangular box around in her hands and peering at it in complete bemusement.

I snatched it away from Sasha. "A twelve-inch monster!" I'd gotten the toy for my bestie for Christmas before she'd gone and gotten herself engaged to Brad while away on a skiing trip over Christmas.

"Why would I need a dildo?"

I gave her a look. "Why would I give the woman who *not only* has a drawer *full* of sex toys, but a whole section of her closet devoted to the vibrating, titillating, orgasm-inducing objects, a new dildo? PS, I used titillating in a sentence." I held my hand up for a high-five.

With that same look of bemusement on her face, Sasha leaned over and smacked her palm against mine. She took the box back from me and stared at it. "I shouldn't need this now. Not with my fiancé being able to do its job…" she grinned, "… and then some."

Taking the toy from Sasha's hand, I dropped the box onto the cushion beside me and took her hands in mine. "I'm so excited for you, Sasha. A little blind sided I have to admit, but still super pumped that you're finally getting your happy ending."

Then I laughed.

Because I couldn't help myself.

She threw a cushion at me.

"Hey!" I said, rubbing the side of my face.

"That's what you get for having your mind in the gutter."

"I think you'll find it's always in the gutter," I shot back, indignantly. "Besides, you try living with an incubus and tell me how much you *don't* think about sex. I'll save you the trouble and tell you that it's about one hundred and ten percent of the time. I feel like I'm a teen boy who just found his daddy's stash of porn under the bed."

She picked up the cushion and placed it in her lap, stroking the face of the unicorn stitched into it. "So, things between you are good?"

"They're great. More than great." I brushed at the knees of my jeans. "You were right."

She cupped her ear. "I'm sorry, can you repeat that?"

I snorted. "I said, you were right. About me. About Sawyer. About my true feelings. About him being a supe and not human. You were right. And so was Sawyer."

She pumped a fist in victory.

"So there. I like Sawyer. I may even more than *like* Sawyer. And bonus, we're kind of irrevocably tied now, anyway."

At this statement, my friend's brows rose. "Yeah?"

"Yeah." Slinking forward in my seat, I grabbed the mug of coffee off the table and took a sip. "I'm his consort?"

"Why did you phrase that like a question?"

Because I wasn't sure how she'd react. Sasha always had my back, always wanted the best for me, but I wasn't sure she'd support *this*. Sex was one thing. A life-long connection with a near-immortal supernatural creature was quite another, and who knew how long I was supposed to live. Sawyer had said an incubus's consort was supposed to be a supernatural too. Clearly, I wasn't, but did that mean when I died in however many years from now that Sawyer would die too?

"Cat? Hello, Earth to Cat?" Sasha snapped her fingers in front of my face, jolting me from my thoughts.

"Hey. Yeah. Sorry."

"You're his consort?"

I let out a breath, nodding. "We're just a little unsure how that works on account of me being human and all."

"What does *being* an incubus's consort mean, anyway?"

I lifted one shoulder in a small shrug. "I'm the one person who can stop the drive to constantly feed off other people."

"He can't feed off other people *at all?*"

I took another sip of my coffee. "He can still feed off the lust of others, but he can't, you know…" I made the finger-in-the-hole gesture and shrugged. "Fuck them."

She shook her head. "You're so crass. Besides that, how was Sawyer also right?"

"He said I was afraid to let anyone else in because I thought they'd disappear from my life again."

Sasha's expression softened. "Oh, Cat."

I waved off her concern. "I'm fine, but it did get me thinking. What if he was right, and I was keeping my heart locked down? So, I decided to just… try."

"I think that's awesome. But if he hurts you, so help me, Cat, I'm going to chase him down and cut off his dick. With an oversized ax because I'd have to go for maximum impact."

I grinned. "You really know where to hit a man where it hurts." My gaze ran over the huge rock on Sasha's finger. Jerking my chin in the direction of her hand, I asked, "How many carats is that thing?"

She seemed to light up from the inside at the mention of her engagement ring. "It's a ten-carat radiant-cut diamond in a platinum setting."

"It's gorgeous, just like the woman wearing it."

Sasha beamed as she continued to stare at the diamond. I'd never seen her this happy before. She'd dated a lot of guys, and by dated, I meant she slept with a lot of guys and rated the size of their dicks in the hope of finding the one who could capture and hold her attention for more than a couple of weeks. She was a smart woman who knew what she wanted in and out of the bedroom, and I was glad Brad was the man to finally win her heart.

"When can I meet your fiancé, anyway? It feels weird that all I really know about him is the size of his dick and that he's loaded."

She laughed, a wicked gleam in her eye. "He's a magnificent eight."

"You should get that on a t-shirt."

"You know what *you* should get on a t-shirt?"

"What's that?"

"Maid of honor."

I cocked my head to the side. "Say what now?"

"Will you be my maid of honor, Cat?"

A very un-Cat-like squeal burst from my lips as I launched myself at Sasha. "Are you serious?" I asked.

"Yes, deadly serious."

"But are you *really* sure? You know how much shit seems to happen to me. I can't guarantee I'll be any good at this."

"You'll be amazing because you're you, and that's all I need." She tightened her arms around me, squeezing. "We'll need to get started on the wedding planning sooner rather than later, though."

I pulled back, shoving some of my teal hair away from my face. "Why?"

"Because we've already set the date, and we want to get married in the spring."

"That's only three months away."

"Four. We're getting married in April."

"Shit. You don't mess around, do you?"

She shrugged happily. "When you know, you know."

"Well, yeah, but I just thought you always said you'd never settle down. That all men were dicks. That they were only good for one thing—"

"I know! But Brad is different. He's sweet and kind and considerate... especially in the bedroom... and I know he's the one for me. Sometimes all it takes is one person to show you the error of your ways."

I scoffed. "Now you sound like a Hallmark card."

Waggling her finger in my face, she chastised, "It'll happen to you one day, too, Cat."

I shook my head, erasing the very thought. Sawyer and I were tied together now, but I didn't want to assume that our connection would turn into anything more than what it was—mainly more about his survival than anything else. I mean, did I want to be with him? Absolutely. I loved the way he worshiped my body, but did I think we would get married and blah, blah, blah happily ever after? No.

Sasha reached for my hand. "It will. Look, if *I* can settle down, then so can you."

I didn't correct her assumption that I wasn't looking for more. If anything, I craved that deeper connection with someone, but being the consort to an incubus was new territory for me. We'd already agreed that if it didn't work out in a monogamous relationship like I wanted, I could date other people, and we would remain friends.

Fuck-buddies but still friends.

Explaining that to potential romantic partners was going to be tricky, though. I doubted there were many men out there who would let their girlfriend fuck another man because she was obligated to keep that man alive.

"… your therapist tonight? It is Friday."

I blinked, refocusing on Sasha. "Sorry, what? I was somewhere else just then."

"I know. I asked if you have to see your therapist tonight? Maybe afterward we could go out for a drink… just the two of us?"

"Oh. Yeah. No, no more therapy for me. Joanna thinks I've got enough coping skills now to not have to see her again."

"Well, that's great, isn't it?"

"I wasn't seeing her because I needed coping techniques. I was seeing her because I was drowning in guilt and anger. Being with Sawyer and the rest of the department has helped, though."

She reached for my hand and gave it a squeeze. "Yep, I totally get that. Did—"

Behind us, the door to the apartment opened and closed. Sawyer's whisky and chocolate scent wafted on the air a moment later. And with that, my pulse spiked.

Sasha turned her head.

"Hot damn, Cat," she muttered. "Why didn't you tell me your partner looked like *that?*"

I'd forgotten that she'd never actually met my partner-come-roommate-come-fuck-buddy.

Sawyer was dressed in running shorts and was bare-chested despite the sub-zero temperatures outside. Sweat ran in rivulets down his chest, ambling casually over his eight-pack and into the waistband of his shorts. I shot to my feet, the movement completely involuntary.

He turned to look at us, his usually gray irises turning dark as he caught the tendrils of our lust. "Pussy cat," he rumbled before flicking his hungry gaze to Sasha. "Aren't you going to introduce me to your friend?"

I shook off the stupor of my flat-out need for him. "Argh, that sounded like a pick-up line. And I will as soon as you put a shirt on. *This...*" I hiked a thumb in Sasha's direction, "... is an engaged woman, and *she* doesn't need to see *all that.*" I gestured to all that deliciousness with a circular motion of my hand.

With a rather boyish grin, Sawyer disappeared down the hall and emerged a few moments later with a shirt on. Unfortunately, him covering himself up did absolutely nothing for my libido. Just catching a glimpse of Sawyer was enough to make me drool.

"Sasha, this is Sawyer, my partner and roommate."

"It's a pleasure to meet you," Sawyer said, swooping in and shaking Sasha's hand.

My best friend actually blushed.

"Dial back on the smoldering, Sawyer," I grumbled. "Your pussy-soaking powers are too powerful."

He flashed me a grin, but even I felt the pressure ease in my body. And I was used to his lust-stoking abilities.

I could only imagine how Sash was feeling.

Which was hot and bothered.

She was fanning herself, nibbling on her bottom lip as if she was thinking of my partner naked. "Well, I'm finally glad we met. Any friend of Cat's is a friend of mine."

I blinked, unsure I'd heard those words correctly. "What happened to cutting off his dick if he hurt me?"

"You were going to cut off my dick if I hurt my pussy cat?" Sawyer asked, one hundred percent aware of what he was doing.

I pulled his face toward me. "You. Stop." I whirled on Sasha. "And *you*? You should be thinking about Brad right now."

"Oh, I *am* thinking about Brad right now," she purred. Sasha stood, scooping up her bag in one swift movement. "And right now, I'm thinking he needs to pay some attention to my lady parts."

"Don't forget…" Sasha swiped up the dildo and shot me a smile, "… your present," I finished. I watched her leave the apartment without so much as a goodbye then turned to look at Sawyer.

The smirk on his face was so smug.

"You did that on purpose." I hiked my hands onto my hips, trying to go for outraged, but the erection tenting his running shorts was too distracting. I licked my lips.

"Did what?"

"Made her want to go get some."

Sawyer closed the distance between us, wrapping his hands around my waist. "And do you want to come and get some because I think I might need your help in the shower?"

"You're incorrigible."

He dropped a lingering kiss on my lips, and I opened for him, tasting chocolate and whisky and the male he was. "I'm insatiable when it comes to you, Cat." Running his hands down my sides, he settled them on my hips and drew me in even closer. "So, what do you say? Want to help me wash my back?"

I rolled my hips against his cock, a soft moan escaping my lips. "Only if you say please," I teased.

"*Please.*" The word came out as a growl, the timbre making me throb between my legs. Damn him and all his abilities to make me writhe. I yelped as he swooped his arm behind my knees and hauled me against his chest. I wrapped my arms around his neck, staring at his profile. His dark hair was plastered to his temples and sweat still trickled down his brow. His gray eyes, although darkening, were still playful, and I was glad I brought out this side of him.

We'd just stepped into his bedroom when his phone began to ring from his nightstand. He growled in its direction, but it didn't stop.

"You have to get that," I told him, attempting to wiggle free of his grip. "It could be work."

"Wolfe gave us the morning off."

Our boss had taken pity on us for working Christmas Day and missing nearly forty-eight hours of our lives. "You know we never stop working."

Sawyer kissed me roughly, nipping at my bottom lip. "You'd rather me take a phone call than be fucked boneless?"

"I'd rather do both, but we're short of manpower right now so stop being a mindless incubus and answer the call."

With a huff, he lowered me to the floor and barked, "What?" After listening for a second, he put the call on speaker, and Vaile Wolfe's rumbling voice filled the room.

"McKenzie, you there?" he demanded.

"I'm here, boss," I said, wrapping my arms around myself.

"I need you two to meet me on my pack's land ASAP." He rattled off an address. "We have a problem."

2

"Well, as far as ominous warnings go, that wasn't so bad," I said as Sawyer ended the call and threw his phone onto the comforter.

He turned to face me—his eyes heavy with lust. "As soon as we're home tonight, I'm going to make you beg."

A shiver trekked over my skin, igniting little pulses of pleasure in my blood. Sawyer was so damn sure of himself, and although I didn't want it to be, it was a…

Total.

Fucking.

Turn on.

"Can't wait. Although, if we are going to the scene of a crime, and let's face it—a call like that from Wolfe *before* work has even begun is a *guaranteed* grisly crime—how in the hell would you be in the mood after seeing all that?"

He stalked forward, anchoring his hands around my hips. "When it comes to you, I'm always going to be in the mood."

Jesus. "*I* need to get that on a t-shirt," I murmured, then he kissed me hard and long, and it was oh-so-satisfying. When he'd finished plundering my mouth like he was going to plunder my body later, he released me.

"Get dressed. I'll meet you at the door in ten."

Stumbling from the room a little unsteadily, I walked the dozen feet to my bedroom and shoved open the door. Despite spending most of my time in Sawyer's bed, I always came back to my room. It was a place where I could disconnect from the whole you-are-my-consort thing. Plus, it contained my new blossoming collection of unicorn statues. I'd asked Sawyer to put up a couple of shelves for me, and he did one better—he set up two new glass-fronted display cabinets and let me have at it.

I'd filled half of one with some of my recent additions and had more coming in the mail.

Thank you, Amazon Prime.

Walking to my closet, I pulled on a pair of black jeans, a black t-shirt, then drew my arms into my red leather jacket. Next, was my motorcycle boots and holster. The gun safe was in Sawyer's room, so for now, it would remain empty. I clipped on the warded cuffs that could hold and subdue any supernatural creature then glanced around for Reaver.

Reaver—the sentient magical sword that seemed to follow me around like a lost puppy. It disappeared when I thought I needed it, became visible when I didn't need it to, and showed up in random places when shit was going to go down. Since it wasn't here right now, I had to assume that some shit was about to go down.

Yippee.

Just the way I wanted to spend my Friday.

Leaving my bedroom, I found Sawyer by the apartment door, waiting for me. His hair was wet from the shower, tiny droplets still clinging to the ends. He was out of his running gear and into his usual work attire—dark slacks and a button-down shirt with the sleeves rolled up to his elbows. His deliciously muscled forearms were on display, and I wanted to lick them so badly.

He gave me an amused smile. "Where are your thoughts right now, pussycat?"

I glanced at him, not even ashamed that he'd caught me ogling. I was his consort. That gave me free rights to ogle.

"Your forearms. They might have a date with my tongue later."

He cocked his head to the side, letting his folded arms fall to his sides. "I think I like the sound of a date with your tongue."

Longing crackled between us, but it was sooo not the time for that. Jabbing my finger at his chest, I said, "You have a one-track mind."

"The same could be said for you," he shot back with a wicked glint in his darkening eyes.

"I'm nothing but a lowly human unable to combat the strength of your lust-inducing thoughts."

Lifting a hand, he touched the opal that lay over my heart. The stupid organ thumped in excitement. "I'm not doing anything, Cat. This is all on you."

The stone around my neck glowed when I was in danger or if there was magic in use around me. It also warned when Sawyer was using his incubus powers on me.

I knocked his hand away with a small huff. "Stop distracting me. We have to get going, anyway. Wolfe will have our heads if we're late because you were feeling frisky."

Handing me my Glock, he said, "I'd have to argue that you were the one who was feeling frisky." He grabbed my truck's keys from the bowl.

My new truck.

Which was an old truck.

At least third hand, but given my luck with trucks and supernatural creatures, I thought this was the most expeditious route. Plus, insurance wasn't going to be paying out to me anytime soon. After my third brand-new truck ended up dragged into Buxton Lake then used to decorate the throne room of the Unseelie Queen in Wonderland, I kind of gave up hope on owning and *keeping* a truck.

Plus, I refused to ride on the back of Sawyer's motorcycle unnecessarily. Even though I'd learned how to ride it in case of an emergency, riding—and possibly dying in a flaming ball on the back of that two-wheeled-death-trap—still wasn't at the top of my list.

"Want to drive?" he asked, holding out the keys to me.

I swiped them from his hand and waltzed to the door. "You can bet your sweet ass I'm driving. Who knows how long I'll have with this one for?"

Sawyer's warm chuckle wrapped around me like a physical caress, making me shiver. Outside, I waited for him to lock the apartment, then we went to the garage in the elevator. The ride down was quiet, but I could feel the charge between us. Sawyer obviously needed to feed, but unless he was literally dying from not feeding, he would always put work before his own needs. He put most things before his needs, and that was one more thing to like about him.

"You're over a hundred and fifty years old, right?" I asked as we glided past the sixth floor.

"Right."

"How long do incubus live for?"

"Thousands of years."

"So, what happens when I kick the bucket and you're left without a consort?"

I was Sawyer's only complete source of food. When I was gone, did that mean he died too? I hated the thought of that, but like him, I was a pragmatist. How in the hell could this continue to work out if I would eventually die?

"I've been thinking about that too," he replied in a soft voice, his clear gray gaze fixed on my face. "I think a little more research is needed."

"Fantastic," I deadpanned. "I love it when you need to research our inexplicable and seemingly unbreakable bond. I love the tension that brings to my life."

Instead of replying to my super valid point, he kissed me on the mouth then turned toward the elevator doors as they sprung open to let us out. The cold air of the underground garage hit me in the face. Winter in Buxton was colder than a polar bear's butt crack, but at least we got the pretty snow.

Walking to my truck, I opened the driver's side door with the key—because my ride was officially older than me—and hopped into the cab. Leaning over the center console, I unlocked the passenger door then turned over the engine. Frigid air blasted through the vents as the beast beneath the hood tried to warm up in all that cold air.

"So where are we going?" I reversed from my spot and navigated toward the exit. The security door trundled up slowly, finally letting us out into the early-morning rush of traffic. "All those directions Wolfe barked at us fled my brain as soon as they entered."

"Get onto the I-90 and keep going. I'll tell you when to get off."

I smirked. "I bet you will."

"Cat," Sawyer warned with a small growl. "I'm on edge now. I wouldn't be pushing me with innuendo." Heat flooded me, setting the blood in my veins on fire. Sawyer reached out and placed his hand on my knee. "I can't wait for this day to be over." He squeezed my thigh then drifted his hand even higher.

I bit back the moan because I couldn't wait for that either. Sawyer was my kryptonite just as much as I was his.

Except I looked nothing like Superman, and Sawyer was too pretty to be Lois Lane.

"Tell me what you know about an incubus and the relationship with his consort."

He blew out a breath but kept his hand resting on my mid-thigh. I forced my mind off the sensation of his fingers on my body, knowing that if we were both naked, he'd be well on the way to making me scream his name right now.

Argh, why was my mind on sex so much?

Sawyer tightened his fingers, flexing them briefly. "I know that an incubus finding his consort has a better chance of winning the human lottery, than getting struck by lightning on the way to claim the winning ticket. I know it's happened so rarely that I've only found a handful of mentions of it in our race's records which have been kept for thousands of years."

"Incubi keep records?" I asked, turning my head to look at him for a second.

"Yes. The scholars of our race like to document the pairings between succubi and incubi when the time for breeding was needed."

"Wow, it sounds *so* romantic," I deadpanned.

"Interbreeding in the race is frowned upon. It's also a danger, so they make sure things are all above board."

"I didn't think sex demons could be so diligent."

"We like to be thorough."

Oh, I just bet they did.

"So, how will you find out more?"

"I may have to reach out to some other supernaturals. There's a race of elves who do nothing but keep the records of all supernatural species' history."

"How are we supposed to find one of those?"

"I don't know," he said thoughtfully.

I let the silence settle then asked, "Do you know when Ben is coming back to work?"

"If I didn't know any better, I'd say you might miss the wendigo."

I shrugged. "I might. His snarling gives me the warm-fuzzies. And who else is going to threaten to eat me for walking past his desk too slowly?"

He shot me a smug smile then looked back at the road. "He's supposed to be back next week."

"We should have a party for him then. Like a welcome-home *slash* you're-not-dead *slash* you-can't-eat-me-now-because-I-saved-your-life *slash* it's-almost-New-Year's party."

"If that's what you want," he replied.

"It is."

He nodded. "Take this exit."

I did as he asked, driving us out into farmland hemmed by forest. I scanned the whited-out landscape around us. "The pack lives out here?"

"Lots of room to run around… far fewer humans."

"Lots more room to maul someone to death too," I added.

He glanced over at me. "What makes you think we're going to a mauling?"

I shrugged. "Just a hunch. The attack on the boy before Christmas couldn't be a one-off thing."

"Or it could've been just that," he replied. "There's a driveway coming up on the right. Follow it to the end."

I pulled off the road and onto a long gravel driveway that wended through the trees until a large farmhouse-style building came into view. Despite looking as if it was centuries old, it had probably only been there a couple of decades. There were hints of modernization in the security cameras and solar panels on the steeply pitched roof.

I pulled to a stop in the turning circle, gazing at the myriad of cars parked around it.

"Who knew Wolfe liked to throw raging parties that lasted into the wee hours of the morning."

"The whole pack lives here," Sawyer said, opening his door and getting out. I turned off the engine and followed him out, taking a deep breath of clear, crisp air.

"Taylor, McKenzie, come with me."

I turned to see Wolfe standing there in a pair of sweats and a wife beater. The guy was stacked… seriously *stacked*. Seeing him dressed as casually as he was, it was like seeing a dog walking on its hind legs—weird, yet fascinating. Our boss turned around and walked not toward the house but toward a cleared pathway that had been made into the fringes of the forest.

I glanced at Sawyer, shrugged, and followed the guy.

As I stepped into the shade of the canopy, the temperature dropped another couple of degrees. And by couple, I meant at least a dozen. I shivered into my jacket, wishing I'd had the forethought to pick up the PIG jacket that was stashed in the back seat of my truck.

Our footfalls were muffled by the snow, so I looked down at the path we were walking on to see that it hadn't been cleared, but it had been used by animals recently—big-ass animals. To avoid potentially messing up the scene, I hopped up onto the bank of snow and passed between two trees.

Then promptly screamed when I went through a spider's web suspended between them.

"Get it off!" I yelled at Sawyer, frantically brushing away the invisible strands that were clinging to my face and neck. I could feel them *everywhere*. With my heart racing, my mind instantly wandered into the *what-could-happen* territory, where I pictured the spider coming out and biting me for ruining its web. When Sawyer didn't come to my rescue, I pulled out my Glock and swung it around, trying to get the spider in the crosshairs.

Sawyer was suddenly there, his large hand coming to rest on top of my gun and pushing it down out of the way.

"It's okay, pussy cat." He was smiling at me. "It's just a spider's web."

"Easy for you to say," I shot back, still frantically brushing away the silk. "You weren't trapped in its clutches."

"I'm quite sure it doesn't have clutches." He re-holstered my gun. "You just flew into panic mode."

"I don't like spiders."

Understatement.

I *hated* spiders.

Shuddering, I said, "Say something to distract me."

"Okay," Sawyer started. "Are you serious about the New Year's party?"

"Definitely. We can invite all my favorite people, and because I'm so selective with my friends, it'll be a short list."

I stopped talking when the smell of snow and clean air was replaced by a faint metallic hum. Vaile stepped to one side, and I saw the source of that smell.

There was a body in front of a dead campfire…

… torn apart.

3

⬥━━━━━━━━━━━⟨≋⟩━━━━━━━━━━━⬥

"That kind of gives new meaning to the words *weenie roast*." I stepped a little closer to the body, my brain trying to play catch-up with all the gore. And the blood. And the things that should've still been on the inside of a body.

"We found him just before I called you," Vaile told us, bending down to look at the prostrate torso positioned perpendicular to the fire.

"Any ID on the body?" Sawyer asked, joining him in the squat-and-peek on the snowy ground.

"Haven't looked yet. Wanted you and McKenzie here. The guy is human, but his attacker isn't. It's definitely a case for PIG."

"I really appreciate your thoughtfulness," I told him as I peered into the blue tent that had been pitched a dozen feet from the fire. The nylon was intact, the zipper on the door pulled down to reveal two sleeping bags, side-by-side. There were also two snowmobiles parked together. "Where's the other guy?"

Wolfe turned to look at me with gray eyes eerily like Sawyer's. Except, in Sawyer's eyes I saw warmth and compassion. In Wolfe's, all I saw was wild untamed savagery. "We haven't looked yet. I told my pack not to disturb any more of the scene considering what we're dealing with."

"And what *are* we dealing with?"

"A shifter... a werewolf. I'd recognize that bitemark pattern anywhere." Wolfe pointed, and I walked over to see what all the fuss was about. The bite was on the victim's face, and I tried to ignore what I was really looking at. If I thought about it too hard, I was sure I wouldn't be able to look at ground beef again without thinking about this poor bastard.

Covering my mouth and nose with the back of my hand, I said, "What are the signs of a werewolf bite?"

"We have larger incisors as well as more inter-incisor teeth in the front. Our molars are bigger and more spaced, and we lack a wild wolf's final molar."

I blinked at the guy then asked, "Okay, so we're dealing with a werewolf. Is it one of yours?"

He growled in response.

Guess not.

After Zachary Hayes' death just over a week ago, this new victim was an unwelcome one. I'd never heard of a serial-killing werewolf before. Serial-killing fae? Naturally. Sociopath witches. Yup. But not this.

I looked over at Sawyer. "Are you thinking what I'm thinking?"

Please say 'It's time to take over the world!'

"We need to find our victim's companion and see if we have to make this a double homicide."

Damn. "I'll go and scout out around the perimeter. You call in the team, I guess."

The team was a very human CSI that collected evidence and photographed the scene. We'd been begging to get a supernatural equivalent, but we hadn't even been able to get our own unmarked cars, so I didn't hold out a lot of hope.

"Do you have Reaver with you?" Sawyer called as I stepped away from the campsite.

"It'll show up when I need it," I called back. "I hope," I said to myself as I stepped over a log and into the forest. The snow was deeper here, hiding all sorts of tree stumps and roots. On my next step, my leg sunk about a foot into the snow. I took another step then dragged out the first, shaking off the snow.

A branch snapped behind me, and I spun around, nearly losing my footing as a terrified squeak escaped my lips. Slapping my hand over my mouth, I stared at the giant black wolf watching me with unblinking citrine yellow eyes. Its fur was thick and shaggy, its head coming up to my chest.

Swallowing my fear, I hissed out of the corner of my mouth, "*Sawyer.*" I didn't dare take my eyes off the hulking animal in front of me. "Sawyer!"

"It's Brax," Wolfe's voice boomed across the short distance. "He's going to follow behind you, so he doesn't disturb the scene. If the werewolf who did this is still out there, I want you protected."

Made sense. I just wished they'd told me that before sending an overgrown guard dog my way. I studied Brax's furry face. "Is it really you in there?"

His tongue rolled out the corner of his mouth in what I assumed was a smile.

"Well, nobody else would smile at me like that," I admitted with a shrug. Turning back around, I proceeded to clomp through the snow while Brax stepped into my empty footfalls, easily navigating through the trees.

"Of course, you get the easy job, stepping into the holes I've already made," I complained.

Brax shoved his muzzle under the edge of my jacket, touching his cold nose to my skin. With a squeal, I spun, slapping him away. Brax danced back out of my reach, and I could've sworn he was laughing at me.

I jabbed my finger at him. "You'll get yours, fleabag."

He yipped, dropping his forepaws down to the ground and raising his butt in the air, his tail wagging.

"Brax," came Vaile's stern voice, the warning in it stinging my own skin.

Like a switch was thrown, Brax straightened, his expression going blank.

"Come on," I said, turning back around to continue on the path I'd chosen.

We tracked half a mile out into the forest then began walking in an arc around the attack site. A few times, I looked behind me to see

Brax with his nose to the ground, sniffing. I kept my head moving, my eyes scanning, looking for any prints or disturbances in the snow. Each step was arduous, with more snow falling into my boots and soaking through not just my jeans, but what felt like the first layer of my skin.

Finding nothing that would've indicated a struggle or chase had occurred in the first half a mile, we backtracked to the primary crime scene.

"Anything?" Sawyer asked.

I shook my head. "Not that I could see, but I can't keep going like I'm going." Gesturing to the soaked bottoms of my jeans, I added, "I need the proper clothes if I'm going to search the forest."

"We'll bring you some," Wolfe replied, glancing over at Brax, and lifting his chin in a silent command. Brax trotted off back toward the house, his long dark tail swishing past the low-lying branches and sending snow falling to the ground.

"Did you find some ID?" I asked, gesturing to the remains.

"Yep. His name is Adam Scali. Buxton local."

"We need to find whoever Adam was camping with before it's too late. It might already be too late." To Vaile, I asked, "Do you guys have any idea how long Adam had been camped out here?"

"Considering how close to our packhouse he is, I'd say they set up camp sometime after dark last night. We do dusk patrols, and someone would've scented them, or heard the snowmobiles last night if they were close."

"Why were they on your lands? I thought werewolves were pretty territorial."

"We are," he growled.

Clearly the fact that a couple of humans had gotten so close was a touchy subject.

Noted.

Behind me, the sound of stiff fabric being dragged over trees and snow caught my attention. Brax was back and carrying some bright pink snow gear in his jaws. He set them down at my feet and wagged his tail slightly. Following in his wake were three more wolves, all a little smaller than Brax.

Refocusing on Brax, I resisted the urge to pat him on the head and tell him he was a good boy. Even though he totally was.

Picking up the jacket, I held it against my chest. I was going to be swimming in it, but that was nothing new. "I have to tell you, boss, I didn't think pink was your color."

"It belongs to my mate," he snarled, his eyes flashing ice-bluewith his wolf.

I gulped. "Well, she has lovely taste."

Stepping into the ski pants, I slid the suspenders up over my shoulders then put on the jacket too. Next, were the boots, which were fur-lined and instantly molded to my feet.

"I'm going to go out there again, take the search area another quarter mile."

"Brax will follow you. His two sons and daughter will accompany you too."

I looked over at the furry patrollers. "All right. I guess more bodyguards are a good thing."

As I walked past Wolfe, he grabbed my arm and said in a low, graveled voice, "Don't look in the pups' eyes for too long unless you want a fight for dominance on your hands. I know you *think* you're a hard-ass, but the reality is these three could tear you apart without a single thought. Their control over their wolf is strong, but Brax will keep them in line regardless."

"Good to know." I gave him a little wave then continued my exploration.

To Brax, I said, "So, these are your kids, huh?" I gestured with my chin at the three wolves behind him. The two biggest had dark fur like their father, but the third had a shaggy mahogany-colored pelt. All of their eyes were yellow like Brax's. "We'll be chatting about this later, don't worry."

Brax sneezed to show he was listening, and I couldn't resist patting him on the head this time. His fur was a lot thicker than it looked. My fingers sank into it, the finer hairs underneath tickling my palm. He seemed to lean into me for a moment before pulling away.

"You're right. Let's get to work."

Treading as carefully as I could, I took the radius out another quarter mile, scanning for broken branches or any other clues that someone had passed through there. I stopped, though, when I caught sight of…

I shook my head, muttering, "Couldn't have been."

Brax whined and cocked his head to the side.

"I *thought* I'd seen… There!" I pointed at the five-inch-high twig swinging from skeletal branch to skeletal branch.

"Please tell me you can see that," I said to Brax, gesturing at the fleeing twig. Except it wasn't *just* a twig. It was a tiny person that looked to be made of twigs. If that was a thing. Which, clearly, it was since I was looking at it.

Against my chest, my opal hummed a little in warning, vibrating slightly as I gave chase. The four werewolves at my back followed on silent feet until we came to another clearing.

Brax stilled… listening.

Then I heard it.

Tiny squeaks and whistles like a pod of dolphins had suddenly decided terra firma was a better place to set up shop instead of the ocean. I swore if I saw a pod of dolphins frolicking about in the snow, I was going to…

… I didn't know what I'd do since I'd seen, heard, and experienced so much more weird stuff in the last couple of months.

The more I listened, though, the more the squeaks made sense to me… as if I could *understand* it.

Delicious! Delicious! Sooo delicious.

More. Give me more. I want the heart.

Eyeballs are my favorite.

The Forest God is merciful. He knows how we hunger!

My opal pulsed again, amplifying the volume of the speakers.

Out of the corner of my mouth, I whispered to Brax, "We've either just stumbled upon a pod of cannibal terrestrial dolphins or we have a bigger problem."

He tilted his head to the other side like what I'd said hadn't computed. "Cover me."

Before I stepped into the clearing, I did a visual sweep of the woods to see if Reaver had decided to join the party.

It hadn't.

With a sigh, I straightened my spine and began edging my way around to the other side of the fallen log that seemed to be the centerpiece of the clearing. It took a few minutes to get a clearer view of the other side, and when I did, I wanted to slink back the way I'd come.

I'd found the other camper.

At least, what was left of him.

4

Swarming the torso of the victim were four twig-bodied, winged little... things. I had no idea what they were, but they looked like fairies. Although, I'd never known a fairy to eat human flesh.

And they were fouling up my crime scene.

"Buxton PD," I shouted, cringing a little at what I was doing. I was yelling at some sort of supernatural creature the size of a beer can. "Stop what you're doing."

All four of them turned to me at the same time, blood and tiny hunks of meat hanging from between their jaws. Their faces were reminiscent of cherubs—all chubby and rosy-cheeked. Their eyes were enormous, too big for their tiny faces. They varied in color from buttercup-yellow to cool mint-green and every shade in between. Their arms and legs were spindly like twigs, and while some had roots for hair, there was only one who had small leaves and flowers growing in theirs. If I had to say why there was a difference, I would've said it demarcated the sexes.

On their backs were tiny wings made of a fine membrane like a dragonfly's. They were iridescent too, a rainbow sheen winking at me through the weak morning sun.

Their chattering ensued.

Who is she?

What is she?

What does she want?

She smells like an incubus…

The creature who said this sniffed at the air, although how he could smell anything other than blood and meat, I didn't know.

Then, in unison, they gasped.

Werewolf!

At my back, Brax stepped free of the tree line and growled at the little fiends. All four bared their teeth right back, and I had to stifle a smile. It was like having a daddy long-legs threaten you.

What's she laughing at? The one with the flowers in its hair chattered indignantly, folding—her?—thin arms over her chest. Yup, I just saw miniature fairy cleavage.

Why does she have a werewolf with her? asked another, the roots-for-hair swinging gently with the movement of its head. *Who is she?*

"Buxton PD," I told them, and they all stilled.

They all stared.

They all cocked their heads to the side in unison.

Shaking the shiver from my spine, I told them, "All right, it's time to back away from the body. This is a crime scene."

It's breakfast! one of the root-haired creatures chattered back, its yellow eyes narrowing.

"Yeah, well, it's also my job to find out how this poor bastard died. You guys *eating* him isn't helping things along. So… shoo?"

Brax's growling—which hadn't stopped yet—kicked up another notch as he stepped past me. His kids flanked me on either side while the russet-colored one stayed behind, covering all our backs.

The creatures hissed at the wolves threatening to take away their meal, baring those sharp little teeth again. I glanced between the two groups wondering if today's adventure would take me into the wonderful world of refereeing a brawl between werewolves and small, carrion-eating fairies.

I stepped between the two groups, intending to calm everyone down, but Brax leaped in front of me and snapped his teeth close enough to one of the creatures that the draft from his breath rustled the flowers in its hair.

More angry chattering as the three with roots for hair shoved the other creature behind them in a defensive maneuver that transcended species.

Curiouser and curiouser.

Despite feeling like I'd fallen down a rabbit hole and into some strange new land where up was down and there was a talking cat, I stepped up beside Brax to pull him away—*if* I could pull him away— when the tiny male creatures began to swarm his head, taking flight on wildly fluttering delicate wings. Brax yelped loudly and backed away a step, dropping his snout to the ground and rubbing his forepaws on it. After a moment, he lifted his head and began snapping his teeth to close his jaws around one of the others.

Brax's kids came forward and tried to dislodge them from their father, but they attacked them too with dogged determination. More yelps filled the air, and I turned when Wolfe and Sawyer burst through the trees.

"Wood sprites," Wolfe growled, his eyes tracking the little creatures. "How many are there?"

"Three attacking. I think they're protecting their female." I pointed at the wood sprite—*not a fairy, Cat*—with the flowers in her hair perched in a fork in the tree. She was laughing hysterically at what was happening to the wolves. "How can we stop them?"

"We can't. They won't stop until they feel like they're not under threat."

Sawyer looked me over. "Are you okay?"

"Fine," I said, wiping my cheek when a bit of flying snow from the fray hit me. "Brax isn't, though."

Pained yelps and whimpers still broke free of the werewolves' throats, but none backed down. This whole thing was hilarious to watch for the simple fact that these tiny creatures were giving the two-hundred-and-fifty-pound werewolves a beat down. I held back the actual laugh.

Ridicule never helped any situation.

The female in the tree chattered angrily. I gaped at her.

"That wasn't a very nice thing to say," I told her.

She blinked innocently. Said something else. Pointed.

"He was trying to move you guys along before you went all swarm-

and-whirlwind on him."

More chattering. Indignantly this time, but I listened because sometimes that's all you needed someone to do.

"There was another guy camping nearby. We think this guy was his buddy… No, I don't think the forest god left him out for you… Because he was killed by something else, and we need to find out what…"

Sawyer eased up beside me. "Who are you talking to?" he asked in a low voice. Like he didn't want to draw attention to my crazy or something.

I pointed at the female wood sprite. "Her. She said her name is…" More chatter. "Sage. The males were just trying to protect her and the meal they were eating."

Sawyer glanced between Sage and me. Shook his head. "You can understand her? She's only talking in chatters."

"Sure I can. Although *why*, I don't know."

"Tell her to stop them."

"Can you call them off?" I asked Sage. "Maybe we can get you something better to eat than a corpse."

I paused. Frowned.

Well, there were some words I never thought I'd say.

Sage tilted her head to the side as if weighing my words. It was a little creepy having a creature so small stare at me so intently. It was almost like she was trying to figure out where my soft spots were so she could substitute me into the eat-the-corpse game.

"Look, I promise to bring a tasty steak with me next time I come into the forest." Which I hoped was never again, but I wasn't that lucky.

Chatter, chatter.

"All right, I'll make sure I leave it outside for a few days before I deliver it to you." *Gack.* "Now, will you call off your boys?"

Sage nodded... well, *sagely*, and put her fingers to her mouth and whistled. We all covered our ears until the sound drifted away. The three males with her stopped immediately, and I had to give this little female wood sprite props for being such a badass.

"Thank you, Sage," I told her then looked over at my boss, the four werewolves, and Sawyer. "Go ahead. The body is ours."

Sawyer pulled on a fresh set of gloves and took a knee beside the body while Wolfe stayed with Brax and the others, his now ice-blue eyes scanning the forest.

I fixed my gaze on the face of the dead man, finding his eyes had been torn from the sockets already. I flashed a scowl at Sage and her posse as they watched from a nearby tree.

"His wounds are consistent with the other man at the campsite," Sawyer said, ignoring the wood sprites completely. "I think the slash to the neck was what killed him, but it was the slash to the stomach that slowed him down."

There were bits of nibbled flesh around the larger stomach wound where the sprites had got to it. I hoped their tasting plate of corpse hadn't interfered too much with the body and scene. "How in the hell did he end up here, though?"

"He ran. Or he was dragged here."

I studied his arms and legs. There were no tears to his clothing or bloody teeth marks. "Doesn't look like he was dragged."

Sawyer scanned the perimeter of the clearing. "There are some broken branches and underbrush there. See?"

I turned. There was no denying that something big had rushed through in a hurry. "Okay, so our guy ran here. Was this before his buddy's death, during, or after?"

"We won't know until Lee does the postmortem to confirm TOD, but if we were camping and a werewolf came after me, what would you do?"

"Firstly," I said, holding up my index finger. "I'd like to point out that I'd never go camping."

He squeezed the bridge of his nose between his thumb and forefinger. "*Cat.*"

"All right. Keep your shirt on." I thought about it for a moment. "I'd like to think I'd stay and fight, but the reality is, I'd probably run. At least, if I knew you were dead, I'd run."

"Wow," he deadpanned. "You are the best partner *ever.*"

"You know what I mean. If there was no hope that you were still alive, I'd be saving my ass."

"What makes you think you could outrun a werewolf, McKenzie?" Wolfe asked.

"I'm faster than I look," I replied, sullen. "So, this guy ran. Got maybe a little less than a mile away then, *boom!* He's attacked. Killed. Partially consumed." I shivered. *The poor bastard.* "Wolfe, think it's the same attacker as Zachary's?"

My boss crouched beside us and peered down at the body. "Yeah, they look the same, but we'll need Lee to take the proper measurements."

Leaning forward, I went through the pockets of the victim's ski pants and pulled out a worn, leather billfold. Opening it up, I grabbed out the ID and looked at the details on the card.

"Thomas Scali. Different address to the other guy, though. Brothers then?"

Sawyer looked. "Yeah, I'd say so."

"I'm the first to admit I know absolutely nothing about camping, but why would these guys actually *go* camping when it's ten below freezing?"

"We found rifles in their tent. They were probably out here hunting winter whitetails or rabbit."

"The rifles were *in* the tent? Not outside it?"

Wolfe shook his head. "Their attacker surprised them, obviously. They didn't even get a chance to try and protect themselves or jump on the snowmobiles to escape."

"How quiet can a werewolf be?"

Vaile said, "In wolf form, very. Our bodies were designed for stealth."

I tried to piece it all together in my head. The brothers were out camping. The werewolf catches them unaware, kills one brother while the other one escapes. The wolf then tracks down the other brother to finish the job, partially consuming the corpse.

Argh, still gross.

I looked back down at the body.

I guess we had a homicidal werewolf on our hands.

Super.

Sawyer tied a bright orange piece of tape around a tree before we started back toward the camp site.

As we closed in on the pack house, Vaile commanded, "Brax, take your pups and go inside." The quartet hustled through the trees, disappearing from view quickly and quietly. Now I understood just how stealthy they could be.

I was about to ask Wolfe why he'd sent them away when I heard the sound of vehicles coming up the gravel driveway. Lee and the rest of the CSI team had arrived.

We emerged from the forest just as the small convoy of vans pulled to a stop. Lee, the PIG medical examiner and a kind of supernatural called a skin-walker, exited the first van, pushing his glasses up his nose as he greeted us.

"Thanks for coming, Doc Lee," Vaile said, holding out his hand to shake Lee's.

The pair clasped hands. "I'd say it was a pleasure but not under these circumstances. What are we dealing with?"

"I'll let Taylor and McKenzie fill you in. They're the team on the case."

Lee looked at us expectantly, his glasses sliding down his nose.

"We'll take you to the first body," Sawyer told him.

When we arrived at the first scene, Lee crouched beside Adam's body and probed his jaw. "Rigor mortis has set in, so I'd say he was killed sometime between six and eight hours ago." He looked up at me, pushing his glasses a little higher. "You said this was only the first body?"

"Yeah. We'll take you to the other one."

I stood and together, Sawyer, Lee, and I walked through the

snowdrifts to the other scene of the crime. The wood sprites were gone when we arrived, but they'd stayed true to their word and hadn't eaten anything more.

"Wood sprites?" Lee asked as he saw Tom's body.

"How'd you know?"

"They like to eat eyeballs. Their hands are so small, their fingers so nimble, they can remove the whole thing without disturbing the optic nerve."

I shuddered. "They were swarming the body when I came across it. Then they attacked four werewolves."

Lee peered up at me from his spot beside the body. "Oh, yes, the venom in their teeth is quite painful to a werewolf."

"So, what do we have?"

"Vaile was right. The bite mark pattern is the same. It was a werewolf, but I'd have to cross-reference with Zachary Hayes' injuries to confirm one hundred percent that we have the same attacker."

"How long will that take?"

He pushed the glasses up his nose. "At least a couple of hours. I'm getting cases from other PIG departments in the surrounding counties which is taking up a lot of my time, but I'll make this case my priority."

"Thanks, Doc."

5

After leaving from the Helheim pack house, Sawyer and I stopped to get coffee before heading into the precinct.

"All I'm saying is life is a soup, and I'm a fork," I told him, taking a sip from my 'glamorous AF' travel mug and placing it on my desk while I took off my jacket and draped it on the back of my chair. "Or is it life is a Jell-O, and I'm a drinking straw? I always get confused."

He shook his head at me. "Where do you come up with this stuff?"

I sniffed. "I can be deep."

"Yeah, you're about as deep as a puddle, pussy cat." Sawyer's phone rang. "Taylor," he answered. "Yep… yep… okay. Thanks for letting me know, Doc."

"That was Lee?" I parked it in my office chair and wiggled the mouse to wake up my computer. It felt like we'd been working for hours already even though it was only a little after eleven in the morning.

"Yeah. He confirmed the brothers were murdered by the same person who attacked Zachary."

"We have a furry serial killer on our hands then?"

"I guess so."

"Taylor, McKenzie, with me!" Wolfe barked as he walked past our office door.

Surprised to be yelled at so unexpectedly, my arm flung out, knocking my coffee cup over. Sawyer caught it before it could hit the floor, righting it on my desk once more.

"You're my hero."

"For saving your new travel mug?"

I snorted. "For saving my coffee."

"*Now!*" Wolfe roared, passing the door once more.

"I guess we're needed."

"How can you tell?" I deadpanned, standing and swiping up my coffee. "What do you think is going on?"

"I don't know."

When we stepped through the door into Wolfe's office, I saw Brax was already there. He grinned at me like his wolf had earlier this morning.

"Oh, Brax, what big teeth you have," I said, making him smile wider.

"Sit. Now," Wolfe demanded, already pacing behind his desk.

I sank down into one of the chairs and waited.

"I want Brax working with you on this case." His sharp gaze swung to Sawyer. "And before you start telling me you're fine, Taylor, save your goddamn breath. You need an expert on this."

"I agree, sir," Sawyer told him. "Having a werewolf investigating makes sense."

"Fantastic. I'm glad you agree with my orders," Wolfe replied, sarcasm dripping from his words. "Brax, to get you up to speed, this is what we know so far. We're now up to three victims, all found in or around Buxton Forest. All vics are male aged between twenty-four and thirty-five. All were killed from a slash to the neck, although they were slowed by the stomach wound first. All vics were mauled and/or partially consumed. Did I miss anything out?"

I raised my hand. "All of them will require a closed-casket funeral."

Wolfe stared at me blankly before continuing, "What we need to figure out is who's doing it and what's their motive." He slammed his fist onto the desk, making me jump. "How many more people are going to get killed before we nail this guy's ass to the wall?"

"I say between three and five." I looked at Sawyer and Brax. "You guys want to start a pool?"

Again, I got a look of consternation from Wolfe. I unfolded my arms, leaned forward, and grabbed my coffee. "Forget I even mentioned it," I grumbled, taking a sip.

"Lee called just before," Sawyer said, taking Wolfe's focus off me. "He confirmed we're dealing with the same werewolf who attacked Zachary Hayes. He's definitely not a wolf you recognize?" Sawyer pressed.

Wolfe shook his head, placing his large palms down onto the blotter and leaning forward. His bulk was intimidating. "No. I track for my pack, and it's not one of ours. Our best guess is it's either a rogue wolf, a newly Bitten wolf, or just some fucking asshole who wants to stir up some trouble because their lives are just too fucking boring." He finally sat, slamming his elbows onto the blotter. "You need to find them and find them fast. Am I understood?"

"Yes, sir," Brax replied.

Sawyer nodded sharply.

I couldn't help myself. I saluted him.

Leaning back in his chair, the steel and leather groaned with his weight. "Some money has been freed up in the budget, and I've secured PIG a paranormal CSI team. You'll call them the next time we have a body." Wolfe slid a card with a number scribbled on it over the desk to Sawyer, who glanced down at it quickly.

"Is there anything else we need to know before we head out?" Sawyer asked.

"Yeah. We're getting new recruits."

My stomach clenched. "Say what now?"

"How many?" Sawyer asked.

"Three… for now." He turned his hard eyes on me. "And you'll be happy to know there was just enough money left in the budget to get work vehicles."

I pumped a fist. "Yes! No more getting my truck totaled!"

Wolfe was about to yell at me again when his phone rang from the corner of his desk. Yanking the receiver up, he held it to his ear and listened for a second. A moment later, he fixed his eyes on Sawyer, Brax, and me.

"Understood. Sending someone over." He hung up. "New body found. Buxton Forest Lodge. Get over there to confirm what we're dealing with."

6

The midday sun was sitting high in the sky when we pulled to a stop in the parking lot of the Buxton Forest Lodge. Snow decorated the steeply-pitched roof and the tops of the trees, making it look like a picture-perfect winter postcard.

I pointed at one of the trucks we'd parked beside. It had the logo of an out-of-town construction company emblazoned on the side of the doors. "They weren't there before, were they? Neither was that." I pointed at a large section of land that had been cleared off the south side of the building. There were piles of lumber covered in bright blue tarps and a small equipment shed had been erected on the other side of the parking lot.

"You mean before Christmas? I didn't notice it. Maybe the lodge is getting some upgrades?"

"It's going to take more than a facelift to erase the fact that they've had a grisly murder here."

There was a sudden *thump, thump, thump* on the window. Brax peered in. "Are you guys getting out or what?"

"Yeah, coming now," I called back.

Brax grinned. "That's what she said."

I opened my door and slid out of the cab, shivering a little as a large gust of arctic wind swept through.

"You want your jacket?" Sawyer asked, reaching into the back seat.

"Are you with PIG?" someone called. We all looked to find a middle-aged woman in sky-high heels, a pencil skirt, and a puffy North Face jacket sliding down the icy path that led to the lodge's doors.

"Yes, ma'am," Sawyer said, handing me my jacket. "Are you Ms. Fraser?"

"Call me, Betty. Please." She shoved some dark hair from her face. "I'll take you to Ms. Peters now."

We followed her up the path and into the warmth of the rustic yet beautifully decorated lobby. Directly in front of us was a reception desk made of rough-hewn planks and a solid maple counter. To the right was a sweeping staircase and concierge desk, to the left a bar. In the center of the reception space was a large rug in reds and browns that sprawled out in front of the river-stone fireplace. Brown leather armchairs were positioned to face it, a small table on each side.

"Ooo, this is nice," I said, passing the fireplace on the way to reception.

"Focus, pussy cat," Sawyer said.

"I *am* focused. I'm multi-tasking," I replied.

Betty led us past reception and through a side door that connected to a covered walkway. Half a dozen cabins spread out before us, each facing the forest. Bright afternoon sun bathed the established holly shrubs that had been planted for privacy between the cabins.

The overall ambiance was severely disturbed by the sheet that had been strung up around the porch of the last cabin.

"The housekeeping team found her when they attempted to clean her room," Betty explained hastily, her blue eyes darting around to make sure we weren't being watched by other guests. Brushing aside the sheet, she ushered us into the crime scene.

The door to the cabin was slightly ajar, the housekeeping trolley askew at the bottom of the porch stairs. Sawyer handed me some gloves then did the same for Brax. When we were all gloved up, Sawyer nudged the door open with his foot, and I recoiled at the scent of blood that rolled out. I glanced over at Brax to find his eyes flashing yellow for the briefest second.

"We'll need to speak to whoever found the body," I told Betty. "Do you know where they are now?"

"In the break room. I'll arrange for it to be emptied so you can speak in private." Betty spun around and hustled out of there.

Not that I could blame her.

Murder did have a way of making people run for the hills.

I turned back to the room. Brax was scanning the space for clues while Sawyer was crouched beside the bed. Sucking in a deep breath, I stepped inside too and shut the door behind me.

The hardwood was slick under my boots as I walked into the expensive room now decorated in shades of red and gore.

Ms. Annabelle Peters' death hadn't been painless.

It hadn't even been clean.

There were pieces of her everywhere.

"Same wounds as the other victims," Sawyer announced matter-of-factly. "More than partially consumed. It looks like she put up a struggle, though. She's got defensive wounds on her arms."

"Ah, I don't want to point out the obvious here, but hasn't the MO also changed? She was killed in this room, right?" I glanced down at the blood spattering the hardwood. "How is that possible if it's a werewolf?" Turning to Brax, I asked, "I guess opposable thumbs aren't something you guys have when you're in your other form?"

He shook his head. "Nope."

"Plus, she's the first female victim." I took another look around the room, tapping my chin with my finger. I checked the window lock, looking for any forced entry then checked the lock on the door. "I'm going to go and speak to the housekeeping staff. You guys good with that?"

"We've got it under control," Sawyer said.

Outside, I found Ms. Fraser hovering anxiously.

"Can you take me to the break room?" I asked. The other woman nodded, although it was a jerky movement, like she was a doll whose stitching was coming loose around the neck.

Pushing through the privacy sheet, I was led back into the main building of the hotel, behind the reception desk, and into the back of house area. There was a short hallway with only four doors. Two of them had signs designating them as the male and female restrooms while another said 'Manager.' The final door was opened and revealed a small break room with an equally small table in the middle, and two couches against the walls.

There was a woman sitting at the table, a cup of coffee in front of her. She was staring—unfocused—into the middle distance, her hands in her lap, her shoulders slumped. I eased into the seat opposite her, looking down at her name tag pinned to her uniform.

Roseanne.

"Roseanne?" I asked, softly at first before raising my voice slightly when she didn't react. "My name is Officer Cat McKenzie. I'm the human liaison with PIG—the Paranormal Investigative Group. I'd like to ask you some questions about what happened to Ms. Peters."

Roseanne's brown eyes shifted slowly to my face. "She's dead."

Yeah, all right, so we weren't dealing here. It wasn't like I could talk, though. The first murder I was witness to, I froze like a deer in headlights.

"Yes," I replied slowly. "She is. And if you have any information about what you saw or heard, you'll be able to help me find her killer. Do you want to do that, Roseanne? Do you want to help Annabelle?"

The woman studied me with watery eyes. Her uniform's formerly crisp white collar was smudged with dirt and a smear of blood. "Yes."

"Good." Pulling out my phone, I tapped into the recording app and started a new voice clip. "Interview with Roseanne…" I paused. What the hell was her last name?

"Bason," Roseanne supplied with a sniffle.

"Roseanne Bason. Housekeeper at Buxton Forest Lodge. Are you ready to start?" At her nod, I asked, "What time did you discover the body?"

"It was around ten this morning." Sniffle, sniffle.

"How did you get into the room?"

"Housekeeping has a master key."

"How many master keys are there?"

"Three. One for the manager and one each for me and Bernadette, the other housekeeper on staff."

My brows rose. "You only have two people on staff in housekeeping?"

"We have less than a dozen rooms. Two is sufficient."

"Where is Bernadette now?"

"I… I don't know. I'm sorry."

"That's all right. Ms. Fraser will know where she is. So, you think you can walk me through what happened this morning?"

She let out a shaky breath. "Okay. Ms. Peters' room is in the wing I look after. I knocked, but when there was no answer, I opened the door and stepped into the room. I smelled the… b-b-blood first then saw Ms. Peters lying on the bed. I ran from the room and told Ms. Fraser, who called the police immediately."

Drumming my fingers on the table, I asked, "The door was definitely locked?"

"Yes."

"How about the window? Was that locked too?"

She furrowed her brow. "I… ah… I don't know. I didn't check."

"When was the last time you were in that room?"

"Yesterday at around the same time." Roseanne ran a hand through her honey-blonde ponytail.

"And everything was fine then?"

"Yes. I saw Ms. Peters go into the room after I'd cleaned."

It was clear Annabelle had been killed sometime within the last twenty-four hours, but what I didn't know was how the werewolf had gotten into the room. Had Annabelle let it in, or had it snuck in? And if it had snuck in, it stood to reason that it could sneak right back out again.

"She didn't bring someone to her room?"

Roseanne wrapped the end of her hair around her finger and twisted. "I don't see all the guests throughout the day. If she did take another guest into her room, she was well within her rights to do that."

"What if they weren't a paying guest?"

"Well, no. If she'd brought someone in from the outside, that would be against the rules of the resort."

I thought back at the layout of the cabins. "Getting someone in would be easy. They could just open the door and let them in. There's enough cover from the privacy planting, and cabin six is the last in the row. There's open forest about twenty feet away."

She bit her bottom lip. "I suppose."

I hit the stop record button on my phone. "Thanks so much for chatting to me. I won't keep you any longer, but if I think of anything else, can I give you a call?"

Roseanne nodded but remained seated, wrapping her hand around her now-cold cup of coffee. After sliding my business card across the table, I stood, finding Betty standing in the doorway of the office.

"Is Roseanne okay?"

"Yes. Scared but okay. She mentioned another housekeeper… Bernadette?"

She nodded. "Bernadette Blakely. She said she didn't want to stand around and do nothing, so she started cleaning some rooms on the other side of the main building. I can take you to her if you like?"

"That'd be great."

She led me into the other wing of rooms, stopping at cabin number eight. A cleaning cart was parked to the left of the door.

"Bernadette, the police would like to speak with you," Betty announced as she led the way inside.

A young woman no older than twenty-two glanced up from the bed she was making. Her eyes were red-rimmed and puffy, betraying how much this murder had upset her. She cast her gaze over me and nodded tightly.

"Hi. I'm Officer McKenzie... Cat. Do you mind if I record this conversation, Bernadette?"

"No, I don't mind." She settled onto the end of the bed she was making, holding her shaking hands in her lap.

Glancing around, I noticed a straight-backed chair tucked under the writing desk in the corner. Retrieving it, I tapped into my voice recording app and sat down.

"Interview with Bernadette Blakely. Housekeeper at the Buxton Forest Lodge. Bernadette, can you tell me about what happened here this morning?"

"One of our guests was found dead in her room. That's all I know. The other housekeeper, Roseanne, looks after that wing."

"But you have access to the rooms in that wing, correct?"

"Right, but Roseanne also has access to mine. We have master keys."

"And where is yours now?"

Standing, she wandered to the cart and pulled open one of the bottom drawers. She pulled out a lanyard with a digital swipe card on it, along with half a dozen keys. Handing them to me, she took her seat on the bed once more.

"Do you always keep the key there, in the cart?"

Her brown eyes darted to Ms. Fraser before she dipped her chin and stared at her hands. "Yes, but I know we're not supposed to."

"It's a security issue," Betty supplied disapprovingly.

"I'm sorry, Ms. Fraser. It just gets in my way when I work."

"Bernadette, do you think someone could've taken your key without you knowing it?"

The girl frowned. "I don't think so. I always take it back to the office after my shift. We generally clean when we know most guests are out to breakfast, at the spa, or on a nature walk."

I studied the credit-card-sized plastic. "How long does it take to clean a room?"

"If it's not a vacate, twenty minutes tops. Vacated rooms require more time… between thirty and forty."

"And this hasn't gone missing in the last week?"

"No. Never."

Key replication was looking less and less likely because it took time, and because the key was in constant use, it would've made it difficult for anyone trying to create a copy.

"Thank you, Bernadette." Reaching into my pocket, I pulled out my card and handed it to her. "If you think of anything else, just give me a call."

I FINALLY FOUND MY WAY BACK TO CABIN SIX WHERE SAWYER AND BRAX were waiting outside the room.

"The photographer is here," Sawyer said. "Did you find out much from the housekeeper?"

"Annabelle was killed sometime in the last twenty-four hours. The housekeeper said the door was locked when she knocked this morning. Three people are in possession of master keys... the two housekeepers and the manager."

"Have any keys been reported as missing?"

"None. No opportunity to make copies or hack it either." Jerking my chin in the direction of the cabin door, I asked, "Did you call in the new team?"

Sawyer nodded. "Yeah. They're elves."

Elves? "Do you think they might be able to help with..." I darted my eyes toward Brax before saying, "... that *thing* we were discussing earlier."

"I already know you two are fucking," Brax drawled. He tapped his nose. "You can't hide shit like that from a werewolf."

"Your daughter and her boyfriend must hate you," I shot back. "And we're sooo not fucking." I gestured between Sawyer and me. "Why would you think that? I don't even like the guy."

"Pussy cat, stop. You're rambling... a dead giveaway that you're lying." Humor laced Sawyer's voice.

I slugged him in the arm then shook out my knuckles. "Shh, I totally had him convinced."

"No, you didn't," Brax interjected. "You two are screwing, and I don't care. Ben knows, too, FYI. He doesn't care either. What we can't figure out is *how* you're doing it."

"Well, Brax," I started slowly. "When a man and a woman are attracted to one another, and they want to show their affection physically—"

"Stop," he replied, holding up his hands. "What I meant is Sawyer can't sleep with the same woman twice, so how in the hell does this whole thing work?"

I looked at Sawyer.

He shrugged.

All right. Up to me how much I want to spill. "I'm his consort."

"Consort?" Brax leaned against the post of the porch and crossed his arms. The light from the fixture on the wall cast a warm glow on him. His eyes flashed gold as his wolf looked out. "Kind of like a mate?"

"Kind of. I guess." Jerking my thumb in Sawyer's direction, I added, "He can't get it up for another woman... only me."

"You have such a way with words," Sawyer muttered under his breath.

"And you agreed to this?" Brax asked.

"It wasn't a matter of agreement, Brax. It just... happened."

"It just *happened?* Man, that excuse didn't work when I was a teenager, and it sure as shit doesn't work now."

"We're hardly teenagers," I protested.

"I'm just surprised Cat accepted this. I thought she hated supes."

"I didn't say I *hated* supes," I hedged, pulled at the stray hair on the bottom of my shirt. "I just had a very strong dislike for them."

Brax grinned. "Couldn't have been that strong."

I slashed my hands through the air, stopping the conversation before I fell into a supe shame spiral. "Okay, Sawyer and I are a thing. He's amazing in bed, and I appreciate a man who knows how to satisfy a woman. I'm hardly any maintenance at all, and all he has to do is feed my unicorn collection addiction because that thing is a *beast*. And PS, I don't care what you think. I'm getting amazing Os."

Brax made a gesture like he was zipping his lips together and throwing away the key. With a smirk on his face, he said, "Consider me properly chastised. And for the record, nobody cares about what you do in your personal time."

"Well... good," I replied, turning around when I heard the door into the lobby open. "We need to stop talking about this because here comes Lee."

Lee pushed his glasses up his nose and gave a little wave as he approached. Over his ubiquitous white lab coat, he wore a thick winter coat that looked to have been made from hundreds of patches of fabric like a quilt.

Maybe he had *made it out of a quilt...*

"Are your ears burning, Doc?" I asked.

He shuffled on his feet. "Err, no."

"Well, they should be." I gestured to the open the door. "We have a humdinger for you."

"Did you just use *humdinger* in relation to a murder investigation?" Sawyer mused behind me.

Turning, I shoved my finger into his chest, wincing when I jarred it against his rock-hard pecs. "Shut it, incubus, or no sex for you later." I shook out my hand. "Owww."

"You can't back that up, pussy cat," he growled into my ear.

I turned to glare at him. "Don't even think about it. Mind on the murder. Not in the gutter."

Following Lee into the room, I found a couple dozen little yellow plastic alphanumeric stands littering the room—markers for the forensic photographer to follow. There were two elves standing off to one side—one with a tablet in her hand and the other with a sketch pad, the pencil gripped in her fingers moving swiftly over the paper. They were both tall, willowy, and blonde. Another elf with a DSLR camera looked like the other two, so I had to assume blonde hair and green eyes were par for the course with the elves.

Or I was dealing with triplets.

Lee cleared his throat, and three green-eyed gazes landed on us briefly before returning to their work. He snapped on a pair of gloves and got a closer look at what was left of Annabelle. Taking a pen from his jacket pocket, he probed under some loose flaps of skin then opened her mouth, shining a penlight into it.

"She's missing a tooth," he said, glancing up. "See."

Sawyer and I stepped closer to take a closer look. "Pre or postmortem?"

He motioned over the photographer.

"There's no blood so post, I'd say."

"What would a werewolf want with a woman's tooth?"

"Maybe a trophy?" Brax asked, coming to stand beside us. "I've heard some killers do that."

"The other victims had all their teeth, though, right?"

"Yeah, but maybe he was disturbed before he could take the

souvenir? Or maybe it's a gender thing? Also," I added. "Is the idea of an opposable thumb in wolf form still outrageous?"

"Yeah," Brax replied. "The only way he could've removed the tooth would be if he shifted back to do it. That might play into the theory that he didn't take the teeth of the other victims because he didn't have the time. Shifting can be a long, arduous process. Afterward, the body is left raw and racked with pain. He wouldn't have been able to shift back easily either."

"You're saying the guy could've been in here with her for *hours*?"

"It's not an outrageous notion."

"All right, so he kills her in the room, shifts back to take the tooth, then leaves in his human form, and nobody sees him?"

Brax shrugged.

Sawyer rubbed the back of his neck. "Maybe the lodge's CCTV footage can shed some light on it?"

7

We found a flustered Betty behind the reception desk. When I saw she was dealing with a whole line of belligerent guests checking out, I understood why.

"I'm not staying here if there's a murderer on the loose," the man currently speaking to Betty said angrily, slamming his fist onto the counter loudly, making Betty jump.

What an asshole.

"I appreciate that, sir, which is why the lodge is offering full refunds for the remaining nights on your booking." She lowered her eyes to the keyboard, typed in a few things then raised her face back to the man. "Mr. Hart, I've refunded the two additional nights you had booked for you and your lovely wife. I do hope you'll come back one day."

"Not likely," Mr. Hart muttered as he turned and walked toward an elegantly bored-looking woman who had to be the wife.

"I'll be another thirty minutes or so," Betty said. "Can you wait for me in the breakroom?"

"I can handle this, Ms. Fraser," a man said behind us. An older gentleman with salt-and-pepper hair strode forward. He wasn't dressed in the same uniform as Betty, but he did have an air of authority about him.

"Mr. Timmins. Thank goodness you're here." Reaching out her hand, she clasped his like he was offering her a lifeline.

"Dale called me and told me what had happened. I got up here as soon as I could." Mr. Timmins' dark eyes skated in our direction. "You must be with PIG." He held out his hand. "Gregory Timmins. I'm the night manager here at the lodge."

Sawyer flashed him his badge. "Detective Sawyer Taylor. This is my partner Officer McKenzie." I waved. "And this is an associate of mine, Braxton."

Leaning toward Brax, I asked in a low voice, "What *is* your last name anyway?"

He grinned, his eyes sparkling with humor. "I don't have one. I'm like Cher or Madonna."

"They have last names, they just choose not to use them."

"Ditto."

"… we can talk in the break room."

I snapped my attention back to the conversation.

Gregory was looking at Betty, who smiled at the waiting guest and moved away to let the night manager take over.

Betty led us into the back of the house section, wobbling a little on her black pumps. In the break room, she took a seat at the table while Brax and I parked it on the couch facing the table. Sawyer eased into the other chair opposite Betty, pulling out his phone to record the conversation.

"Has Ms. Peters been removed from the room yet?" Betty asked, wiping a finger under her eye.

"Yes, the medical examiner has her now, and we'll be taking great care of her."

"Will you also notify her family?"

"Of course. We'll do that after we finish here." Sawyer shot Brax a look, who nodded. When he turned back to Betty, he placed both his hands—palms down—onto the table. "There was one other thing we'd like to discuss with you."

"Of course." Another tear ran down her cheek, and I looked around for a box of tissues. I stood and retrieved it from the top of the microwave, handing a few to Betty. She took them with a grateful smile and dabbed under her eyes.

"What is it that you need?" she asked.

"It's just a couple of questions. Firstly, did Ms. Peters ever have guests in her room?"

Betty blinked. "Guests as in people not staying at the lodge?"

"Yes."

"No. It's prohibited to have people not registered inside guest rooms."

"But it's possible, right?" I asked. When Betty turned to me and blinked—confused—I added, "To sneak someone in. They could be in the forest waiting?"

"It's incredibly isolated here. I highly doubt someone would come all this way to hide out in the woods in the hopes they'll be admitted into one of the cabins."

Sawyer gave me a look, and I shrugged. That theory was kind of dead in the water, but I wasn't so willing to forget it altogether.

"One last question. We were wondering if you had CCTV working around the lodge? Maybe one of the cameras captured something?"

The woman nodded and stood, scooping up her Kleenex as she did. "Yes, we do have some cameras running. If you'd follow me?"

Dumping the crumpled-up tissues into the trash, she left the break room and led us into the manager's office. It was double the size of the break room with two desks set up, two sets of armchairs placed in front of each respective desk and a large area rug covering the hardwood. Betty moved to the closest desk and woke up the computer.

A few clicks later, the screen was broken into six grids. Each grid had an image of some parts of the lodge, cabins, and exterior vantages. "What time frame would you like to look at?"

"Around this time yesterday, please."

Betty loaded up the footage then clicked *play*.

We all watched as a whole lot of nothing happened—well, nothing that we could see anyway.

I asked, "What's the closest camera to cabin six? Can we just load up that one?"

Betty nodded, her hand moving the mouse around the pad expertly. The next thing I knew, we had a full-screen image of the cabin.

"Play it again from this time yesterday, please?"

Betty stood. "You can speed it up and down if you like. Just use the

Z and X keys to go faster or slower. Hit the spacebar to stop."

I planted my ass into her chair before Brax or Sawyer could. "Ooo, nice," I said, stroking the leather. "Great lumbar support."

"Cat," Sawyer warned.

I flashed him a grin then got to work. I scrolled past most of the evening things. At six, Annabelle went for dinner. She returned at 8:52, weaving a little on her feet. Once she was in her cabin, nothing happened. I sped past the wee hours of the morning until something caught my eye.

"What was that?" I asked, stopping the feed just after the footage flickered, and rewound it. We all leaned in a little closer. "It looks like…"

"A man," Sawyer finished. He looked over at Betty. "Do you recognize him? Is he a guest currently staying here?"

She shook her head. "I've never seen him before."

I rewound the footage. It was hard to get a good look at the guy because there was some sort of electrical interference going on, but what was clear, was the man approached the door of cabin six and was let in.

"Roll forward to see when he exits."

I started the footage again, watching the minutes tick by into hours. I'd almost dozed off when Sawyer barked, "Stop it there!"

I hit the spacebar and stared at the screen. Blinking. "Please tell me I'm not dreaming."

"You're not dreaming," Brax helpfully supplied.

The man, the same man who had gone into the cabin, had come out. His face was covered in blood, but his clothes—worn-out jeans and a plaid shirt over a solid black t-shirt—were clean. I hit the space bar again, beginning the playback. He turned to look in the direction of the camera, and I caught the slash of high cheekbones, caramel skin, dark eyes and pin-straight long black hair. With a flash of a smile, he took one step. Another step. Then disappeared off the edge of the screen.

"Is he one of your wolves?" I asked Brax.

He shook his head. "Definitely not. He could be a rogue. It's not unheard of to have a random wolf without a pack passing through the area. I just thought we would've smelled him by now if it was."

If he wasn't a Helheim wolf, then what the hell were we dealing with?

I rolled it forward again, hoping to see something more. I paused it. Blinked. Wondered if I was seeing things.

"Is it just me, or did that tree just walk up the cabin?"

On the screen, what looked to be an oak tree ambulated on its roots like a human would walk. It was covered in Spanish moss and leaves, which should've been my first tip that we weren't in Kansas anymore. Moss didn't grow like that here—it got too cold. I moved a little closer to the screen in the hope that my brain would figure out what it was looking at, but if anything, I was more confused.

"Sawyer?" I asked in a small voice. I jabbed my finger at the screen. "Is that a walking tree?"

My partner cursed. "No, it's not. It's a dryad."

"A what now?"

"Dryad. A tree nymph."

"Do they like to kill or drown children? Because I don't know how much more I can take of those kinds of supes."

His lips quirked up a little in the corner. "No. They're generally peaceful."

As it got closer, I could see the buxom body of a well-endowed female. She was wearing a bustier made of bark, her pale green skin revealed in the deep V at the top. Her hair was a slightly darker shade of green, hanging like the Spanish moss that covered her legs and arms. Out of her head, two antlers speared through her hair.

The female stood in front of the cabin, watching for a moment, before climbing the stairs of the porch and disappearing inside. Only a few minutes passed before she reappeared, blood covering her hands and arms.

I felt my stomach turn.

"What did she do?" Betty asked in a hoarse voice. "Why is she covered in blood too?"

"We don't know," I said just as softly. And, honestly, the more I found out about supes, the more I wanted to know less.

The dryad returned to the forest and disappeared, and I turned slowly around in the chair, thinking. *What in the hell was happening here?* Had Annabelle's death been ritualistic in nature, or was something far less sinister—like plain bad luck—the reason for her murder?

"Cat, stop the recording," Sawyer barked, leaning over me to hit the spacebar.

Oh, Jesus, what now?

I jerked my attention back to the screen. "What? What is it? What did I miss?"

He pointed to something on the edge, just out of the camera's field of vision. "Not what. *Who.*"

I leaned in a little closer. There was a young girl standing there, staring at the cabin. She couldn't have been any older than thirteen or fourteen. "What is she doing out in the dead of night?"

"Do you recognize that girl, Betty?" Sawyer asked in a gentle voice. "Is she a guest here?"

"Y-yes. She's staying with her family. Their s-s-son was murdered just before Christmas, and the mother, Mrs. Hayes, is refusing to leave until they find out who did it. They're in cabin five."

"Shit," Sawyer said.

"Shit," Brax echoed.

"Think I could get one of these chairs for my desk at work?" I asked, spinning around one last time.

8

"Brax, can you go and notify Annabelle's next of kin?" Sawyer suggested as we left the manager's office. "Then head home to see your family."

"Roger that. I'll see you guys at work on Monday."

"Are we going to see if Mrs. Hayes will let us talk to her daughter?" I asked.

"Yeah."

We walked back outside, climbing the porch steps of cabin number five. Before we could even reach the door, it opened, and a stressed-looking woman dressed in a dark pink velour running suit with matching tennis shoes stood in the doorway. Her brown hair—streaked with gray—was being held hostage in a loose, messy bun at the top of her head.

"Are you here about my son?" she asked without any preamble, her light brown eyes darting between mine and Sawyer's faces.

"Your son is Zachary, right? Zachary Hayes?" I asked, confirming we did have the right family.

Hope flared in her gaze. "Please tell me you have information."

Sawyer shook his head. "I'm sorry, ma'am, but the investigation is ongoing. But there might be something you can help us with on this case."

Mrs. Hayes stepped onto the porch and shut the door behind her. "What is it?" She crossed her arms. "I'll do anything. If you want me to put up a reward, I will. I have a million dollars in cash set aside just for that purpose."

"No, no reward yet." He waved the notion away. "We have some good leads on the case right now, but I'm wondering if we could speak to your daughter?"

She frowned, a deep depression forming between her eyes. "I don't understand. Why would you need to speak to Rachel? She didn't see anything."

"Actually, we think she did," I said. Looking over at Sawyer, I waited for him to give me the go-ahead. "Last night, the woman in cabin six was murdered. We think it's the same person who murdered your son."

Mrs. Hayes gasped, covering her mouth with her fist.

"We checked the surveillance footage, and it shows Rachel outside the cabin around the same time the killer left."

All the color drained from her face. "My baby was outside while that… that… *bastard* was there?" Her legs seemed to give out then, and she dropped into the wood-carved chair beside her. "No, she couldn't have been. I checked in on her myself."

"You checked on her at three in the morning?" I asked.

She blanched. "She was outside at *three o'clock*? In the morning?"

Sawyer nodded grimly. "And if we could talk to her, it would help so much with the investigation."

Mrs. Hayes stared at us for a full minute, the color slowly returning to her cheeks. "No."

"Ma'am?" Sawyer asked.

"*No*. You're not going to drag my only remaining child into this." She rose. "No."

And with that, she turned on her mark-free soles and fled back into the cabin. I pulled a card from my pocket and slid it under the door.

"What the hell was that about? She wants us to find her son's killer, but she doesn't want to help us do that?" Clinging to the railing, I made my way off the icy porch steps and back onto the shoveled pathway. "You know, I just don't understand people sometimes."

"She's lost a son, pussy cat. The mere thought of losing her daughter as well terrifies her."

"Where does that leave us?"

He pinched the bridge of his nose with his thumb and forefinger and let out a sigh. "I don't know. We need to speak to Rachel." He glanced over at the cabin. "Maybe we could try again tomorrow? Perhaps all Mrs. Hayes needs is to sleep on it and see that we're only trying to help her?"

"Maybe you're right." I stared out into the forest not twenty feet from the path. Where in the hell had the killer gone afterward? Was there a trail he used to get here, and would we be able to find it?

"Could we speak to—" I stopped when my gaze landed on a shadow moving alongside the cabin.

"Cat?" Sawyer asked. "What is it?"

Pressing my finger to my mouth, I pointed. Rachel Hayes stepped into the light, her small hands clasped together in front of her. Her blonde hair was hanging loosely around her pixie face, brushing against a spray of light brown freckles across her cheeks and nose.

When there was a loud *bang* and what sounded like shattering glass in the cabin, the girl retreated deeper into the shadows. I stepped toward her, but Sawyer brought me up short by grabbing my arm

"What are you doing?" he hissed into my ear.

"I'm going to talk to her."

"She's a minor. We can't legally ask her question without her parents' permission."

I looked over at the girl, indecision tearing through me. We needed to speak to her, but I wasn't about to circumvent laws designed to protect minors to do that. When Rachel gestured for me, I shook my head and pointed at the cabin. *Not without your mother,* I mouthed, and I saw the hope drain out of her with the fall of her shoulders.

She walked around to the back of the cabin to, assumedly, climb back through the window she'd crawled out of to come and speak to us.

When we were back in my truck, I asked, "What do you think she wanted to tell us?"

"I'm not sure. Something about her brother, obviously."

"Are we going to get another chance with her?" I started the engine of my relic of a truck, finally coaxing it to life with a spluttered roar.

"Honestly, I don't know. Her mother was pretty adamant that she wants her daughter to have nothing to do with the investigation."

"Yeah, but at the expense of finding her son's killer? Sounds like a risk worth taking to me." I shifted the truck into gear and slowly reversed from my spot. "Let's hope Lee comes back with something we can work with. And fast."

9

When I woke up the next morning, there was a voicemail waiting for me. I sat up, hitting play and putting it on speaker phone.

"Officer McKenzie? It's Mrs. Hayes. Lucy." Her voice was a strangled whisper. "Rachel has… gone missing. I don't know where she is. I don't know how long she's been gone. I just *don't know*. I found your card under the door. I need your help. As soon as you get this…" An audible gulp. "Please come to the resort as soon as you can."

I immediately slipped out of bed and dashed into Sawyer's room. "We need to go," I announced, finding him propped up against his pillow, reading.

Lowering the book, his heated gaze traveled all over my body slowly. I glanced down at the tank and panties I'd gone to bed in last night. "*Focus*, Sawyer."

His gray irises were gobbled up by the darkness of his hunger, his need to feed pushing against me like a physical caress, luring me closer.

Take another step this way, pussy cat, it seemed to say. *Let me into your body, and I'll make you feel so good.*

"Rachel is missing," I hissed, taking a step closer.

Just like that, the power of his lust-fueled perusal faded. He shook his head, massaging his brow. "I'm sorry, pussy cat." He looked at me, his eyes slightly glazed. "What did you say?"

"Are you okay?" I asked.

"Fine. I just… never mind."

He didn't need to say it. He needed to feed, although, I wasn't sure why since he'd spent about four hours wringing every last ounce of pleasure from me last night before I'd stumbled into my own bed so he'd leave me alone. He shouldn't be hungry again so soon.

Shaking my phone at him, I said, "Mrs. Hayes left me a voicemail early this morning." I pressed play on the message, listening once more to the frantic voice of a mother who'd just discovered her young teenage daughter was missing from her room. "We need to go. We can call Brax on the way there."

He threw the quilt from his body and sat on the edge of the mattress. Scrubbing a hand over his face, he mumbled, "Don't worry Brax with this. He has a family. He needs to spend time with them on the weekend. We can handle it by ourselves."

I nodded, scrutinizing him. "Are you sure you're okay?"

"Fine," he replied, not looking at me. "I'll meet you in the kitchen in ten."

Something wasn't right—something that teased at the edge of my consciousness—but I didn't know what it was. Retreating to my room, I took a quick shower, then got dressed in black jeans, a black sweater, and my puffy jacket with PIG written in yellow letters on the back.

"Coffee for you," Sawyer said, looking more like himself as he slid my unicorn travel mug over to me.

I took a sip. "I love that you think about my caffeine needs."

"It's for purely selfish reasons. I just don't want to be around you when you're uncaffeinated."

I flipped him off with my free hand.

He nodded at my sidearm on the end of the kitchen counter. "Put that on and we can go."

I glanced around the kitchen. "You haven't seen Reaver, have you?"

"Lost your toy again?" he deadpanned.

"Yeah, my super sharp, sentient one." I was sure it would turn up when I needed it. Bringing the holster over my shoulders, I checked my Glock then slid it into place.

The ride out to the lodge was a long one on account of the icy mountain roads. When we finally reached the top, I parked my truck and stared at the huge stone-and-timber building. Smoke was drifting steadily from one of the two chimneys jutting from the pitched roof.

"What do you think we're going to find?" I didn't want it to be another body—especially if it was a kid.

"I'm not sure, but I think we should be ready for anything."

"Fantastically vague answer. Thank you for that." I opened the door and slid out. The cold wind slapped me in the face, forcing me to burrow deeper into the collar of my jacket. More snow had fallen overnight, leaving the paths that had been clear yesterday covered in a few inches of snow. Moving slowly through the drifts, we entered the lodge, stomping the slush and ice from the treads of our boots.

Mr. Timmins, the night manager, was standing behind the reception desk, his gaze focused on the computer screen. His head jerked up when I slipped on the hardwood floor with a loud squeak. Sawyer caught me easily by the elbow and righted me.

"Detective Taylor, Officer McKenzie, what are you doing here?" Gregory asked with a frown, coming out from behind the desk. He reached for our hands to shake in a two-handed grip.

"We received a phone call from Mrs. Hayes asking us to come and speak with her." I looked around. "Where's Ms. Fraser? I thought she took the day shift?"

"Ah, yes," he replied. "You'll find Mrs. Hayes still in her room. In answer to your other question, Betty doesn't work weekends. Please, attend to Mrs. Hayes, won't you? That poor woman has lost enough already."

Sawyer and I walked through the main lodge and outside onto the covered walkway to the cabins. When we knocked on the door of number five, Lucy opened it quickly. Gone was the woman we'd met yesterday. Today's version of Mrs. Hayes was a woman whose son had been murdered and whose daughter had gone missing.

In other words, she was a dumpster fire of emotions.

"Thank God, you're here," she said, standing back and letting us into her cabin.

I stepped inside and looked around. Like the main lodge, there were large logs and smooth river rocks used in the construction. The rest of the décor wasn't hunting-lodge-chic, but rather Hamptons-style-luxe.

Lucy sank into the cream-colored couch, tears already pooling in her eyes.

Sawyer took a seat in the small armchair while I stayed standing.

Sawyer said, "Is it okay if I record our conversation?"

"Yes, that's fine." Mrs. Hayes smoothed the sleeve of her sweater. "I can't believe she's gone. You *have to* find her."

"And we will," he reassured her. Placing his phone on the arm of the chair closest to Lucy, Sawyer said in a calm voice, "Tell us what happened."

Lucy sucked in a breath and let it out. "Directly after you left yesterday evening, Rachel and I had a big fight. She said..." She sucked in a breath and let it out. "She said she needed to speak with you about what she'd seen. I refused to let her because I was terrified of losing her too, so I told her to go to her room."

Reaching over, Sawyer pulled a couple of tissues from the box on the table between them and handed them to her. Lucy wiped under her eyes and blew her nose softly.

"When I went to check on her before I went to bed, her room was empty, and her window was slightly ajar." She raised her eyes to look at us. "Rachel *knew* not to have a window open at night. I've been fastidious in keeping all the windows and doors shut and locked while we've been here."

Fastidious. I was sure Sawyer was coming in his pants to hear that word used in a sentence.

"What time was it that you checked on her?" Sawyer asked.

"Around eleven."

My partner turned to look at me. Yeah, that's right. That was a whole five hours after we'd left. We already knew Rachel had been outside at six o'clock, but we'd assumed she'd gone back into the cabin after we'd shooed her away.

Dammit, were *we* responsible for the girl's disappearing act?

I swallowed. "Was anything missing from her room? A bag? Clothes?"

Lucy frowned. "I don't..." She pinched the bridge of her nose, squeezing her eyes shut as she did. "I didn't think to check." She stood quickly and rushed into a room that connected to the living room. Sawyer and I followed her in, waiting to see what the verdict was.

"A backpack is missing." Lucy was standing by the desk, staring down at where her hand lay on a scrap of paper. "She kept it here beside the desk."

"Anything else unaccounted for?" I walked over to see what had caught her attention. It was a sketch of something large and black. I couldn't see much more of it because Lucy's palm covered the middle of the page.

She balled her hand into a fist, scrunching the paper up with it. Throwing it into the trash, she shuffled over to the window and stared out.

Leaning down, I picked the ball of paper from the trash and crammed it into the pocket of my jacket. As I was about to straighten, I noticed Reaver sticking out from under a pile of clothes on the floor.

Well, this couldn't be good.

Pulling the sword free, I forced a thought of *disappear* toward it. With a little shiver, it winked out of existence, and my opal flared hot for a second.

"You need to get my girl back." Lucy's voice was hollow. "My husband withdrew from me... said I was obsessed with Zach's death, and he refused to stay here a minute longer." She turned—her face haunted. "My son is dead. I can't lose Rachel too. I just can't."

"We'll find her," Sawyer said gently. "Cat and I will go out and investigate around your cabin. All I ask is for you to stay inside." He rested a hand on her shoulder, and I felt the change crackle in the air. My opal pulsed. "Can you do that, Mrs. Hayes?" he added in his persuasive *let me ravish you* voice.

Lucy got a dreamy sort of look in her eyes. "Yes, I can do that," she agreed, a sexy grin forming on her lips.

"Jesus, Sawyer, dial it back a bit," I muttered under my breath, proud of myself that I didn't feel a single flare of jealousy.

No, really. I didn't.

With my invisible sword in tow, I left Rachel's bedroom and walked back into the main living area of the cabin. Digging into my pocket, I pulled out the picture Lucy had crumpled up into a ball and flattened it out on the kitchen counter. As I smoothed my fingers over the thick art paper, I studied the drawing. It was a wolf—as I'd suspected it would be—but it didn't quite look the same as Brax did when he'd been in his wolf form. Rachel had drawn it with daggers running down its back.

"Cat?" Sawyer asked behind me.

"Come and look at this." Sawyer approached, his chocolate and whisky scent enveloping me. "Found this in Rachel's room. Lucy tried to hide it from us."

He studied the image, his brows dipping low. "It's a wolf."

Running my finger along the daggers along its spine, I asked, "With built-in knives? Seems like an upgrade *not* given by nature. It can't be a werewolf. Brax didn't have these." I tapped the page again. "So, what else could it be?"

Mrs. Hayes walked out of Rachel's room, and I hastily scrunched the drawing back into a ball and shoved it into my jacket pocket.

"I don't know, but we should start our search outside," Sawyer said.

The first place we checked was the side of the cabin, where Rachel had been standing last night. I couldn't see her footprints anymore, except for a partial heel mark under the cover of a holly bush.

"Most of the footprints are gone," I told Sawyer.

He grunted. "Let's work back toward the tree line. Maybe we'll find clearer prints the closer we get to the forest."

I studied the expanse of trees in front of us—an endless sea of skeletal deciduous limbs and evergreen boughs covered in snow. "You think that's where she's gone?"

Please don't say yes. Nothing good ever came from walking into a forest in the middle of winter.

"Yes."

Fuck.

Sucking in a breath, I sent up a prayer that we found Rachel quickly so we could get the hell out of there. But as I walked closer to the trees, it felt like someone was watching me. Peering over my shoulder, my gaze darted from Mrs. Hayes's cabin to the main building. I was expecting to see someone standing by a window that looked out onto the rear of the resort...

... but nobody was there.

Still cautious, I turned and jogged to catch up with Sawyer, who was already a few dozen feet ahead of me.

"Look for footprints, even partial ones, near the base of the trees," he told me when I skidded to a stop at his side. "The snow that fell last night was heavy, but it wouldn't have been able to make it this far down to the ground after going through the canopy."

For what felt like an eternity—but was probably only fifteen minutes—we combed the forest floor looking for anything that would tell us which direction Rachel had gone.

"We need to go in a little farther," Sawyer announced.

I nodded, my shoulders tightening. I glanced behind us. The feeling that we were being watched hadn't gone away, but he was right. We needed to get a bead on where Rachel was, and we needed to do it before night fell. A teen girl might be able to survive one night out in the elements, but I doubted she could survive two.

Sawyer led the way, passing between a pair of trees that were leaning toward each other to form a natural arch. As soon as he emerged on the other side, a thick, curling mist appeared out of nowhere.

"What's with the mist?" I asked, running my hand through it. It curled around my wrist playfully but retreated when my opal pulsed in warning. I looked up to find the mist swarming Sawyer too, only his face was set into a grimace. With a growl, he pulled at the tendrils wrapping around his neck.

"Do you have Reaver?" he asked in a hard voice. At my nod, he said, "Call it up, and don't let the mist stay in contact with your skin for too long. As long as we keep moving, we'll be okay."

There were welts on the side of his neck, already oozing a clear liquid. Swallowing, I summoned Reaver into my palm and held it out in front of me. The blade began to glow bright blue, creating a halo around us.

Together, we inched forward, the mist retreating with each step, but I paused when something bright pink tied to a tree caught my attention.

"Sawyer," I said. "I think I've found something."

He untied the fabric then scanned the trees around us. "It's a scarf... well, at least a piece of a scarf." He handed it to me for a look. "Rachel must've left it here so she could find—"

Reaver began to hum in my hand.

A scream cut the air.

Sawyer pulled out his Glock. "This way," he said, taking off at a run.

"I hope I don't regret this," I muttered to myself then took off after him. I ran as fast as I could, but I kept tripping on tree roots. After the third fall, I twisted around to find the root had wrapped around my foot, like the mist had wrapped around my wrist.

"Cat?" Sawyer yelled from somewhere waaay ahead of me.

"What?" I grumped.

"Where are you?"

"In my mind, on a beach somewhere with a shirtless waiter called Juan who gives me unlimited espresso martinis in unicorn-shaped drink wear."

There was a beat of silence. "And in reality?"

Was he laughing *at me?* That was *definitely* a barely contained laugh in his voice.

"I'm flipping you off and considering withholding sex to punish you for your insolence."

Ha! Take that, Sawyer Taylor.

"Seriously, where are you?"

I heaved a sigh. "On my ass after a tree root tripped me up."

"You mean you fell over it," he said, his voice closer now.

"No, I mean, it *tripped me up.* Three times."

He appeared out of the mist like some sort of sex god…

Oh, wait, he *was* a sex god.

He held out his arm and lifted me. Twisting my foot, I finally freed it from the tangle of roots and glared at the tree responsible.

"Have we stepped into Wonderland without knowing it?" And, yes, that was panic in my voice. Just in case, I did a mental check.

No change in pressure.

No spider-crawling sensation.

No freak-out necessary.

But then another scream rent the air.

I said, "That sounded like…"

"Yeah," Sawyer agreed. "Let's go."

Without letting go of my hand, Sawyer dragged me after him.

Another scream.

Only this time, it didn't stop. It continued on, chilling the blood in my veins.

The mist seemed to grow thicker, and if I didn't know any better, I could've sworn the forest itself was trying to stop us from going any farther.

When we finally pushed through the last of the mist, Sawyer and I were brought up short. Above our heads, stars twinkled in an inky-black sky.

It was night here?

"How could it be…?" The question died on my tongue when I took in the scene in front of me.

The fact that time had seemingly changed was the least of our problems.

10

We'd found Rachel.

Still alive.

Dressed in a pink puffy jacket, blue knitted hat, jeans, and boots, she was sprawled on the ground, her expression set in horror as the dryad we'd seen in the CCTV recording reached for her. Sawyer brought his Glock up to chest height, his finger outside the guard. "Buxton PD. Stop what you're doing."

The dryad turned to us, compassion I didn't expect to see shining in those warm, olive-green eyes. She stood slowly, the moss on her antlers swaying slightly.

"I meant her no harm," she said in a wonderfully lilting voice. "I was just trying to help her."

"Like you helped the other woman at the lodge?" I asked, my gaze darting between the dryad and Rachel, who was now laying still—

probably passed out from the shock of seeing a walking oak tree. There was a gash on her forehead, and one of her legs looked like it had been badly broken.

"I tried to help her too," the dryad replied calmly. Her long dark green hair shifted— the motion like a wild wind blowing through a field of long grass. "I tried to save her life after the wolf attacked her."

My gaze flickered over to Sawyer.

Bingo, I mouthed.

With a grim set to his mouth, he nodded.

The dryad squared her shoulders. "I only try to keep the peace in my forest, and he's caused nothing but destruction."

"When did you find Rachel?"

"A few minutes ago. I heard her whimpering." The tree nymph turned her attention to the young girl. Gesturing to Rachel, she said, "Her leg is broken, I think. I assume the bone is not supposed to peek through the skin like that?"

"It's not. She needs help. We have to get her out of here and to the hospital."

"I was trying to render her some aid." The dryad's sincerity burned in her eyes—in the way she said her words. "Now that you are here, you should take her before the wolf comes to claim her."

"Fantastic idea." Turning to Sawyer, I asked, "Are you able to pick her up without jostling her leg too much?"

He nodded, shooting me a look. I took out my sidearm and held it down by my thigh, protecting my partner as he re-holstered his Glock and bent down.

The dryad watched me with careful eyes.

"I have had enough destruction in my forest," she said. "You have nothing to fear from me."

"It's nothing personal," I said. "I just have a really hard time trusting strange supes."

The dryad inclined her head. "As you wish."

Sawyer curved his hands under Rachel's small body, lifting her carefully. Cradled against his broad chest, she looked positively tiny. To the dryad, I said, "You said you were trying to help the other woman."

"I was."

"This wolf, have you seen it attack any others?"

"Yes, but I was unable to save them either."

"How many?"

"Three. All men. All men who were not harming it in any way."

Confirmation at least that we were dealing with the same wolf.

"We need to go," Sawyer murmured, walking past me and back in the direction we'd come.

After he disappeared through the mist, I asked the dryad, "Will it kill again?"

The dryad took in a deep breath of air, her breasts pushing against her bark bustier. "That, I do not know. The beast has been angered and is looking for his reparation."

"Cat?" Sawyer called.

"Coming!" Turning to the dryad, I added hastily, "Thank you for trying to help her. And the others."

The nymph bowed again. "I will always try to protect innocents in my forest."

I turned and caught up with Sawyer a couple of dozen feet away.

"How's she doing?" I asked, running my eyes over Rachel. All the color had leeched from her face, but at least the gash on her head had stopped bleeding.

"She's doing okay, but we need to get help for her leg."

The mist thinned as we moved toward the edge of the forest, no part of it trying to stick to our skin anymore. My opal pulsed once, and I let out a breath, peering up. The stars were gone, the weak winter sun streaming through the branches. Spinning around, I took another step back into the nighttime forest, then returned to the 'daytime.'

I shook my head. "Well, that was the freakiest thing I've ever seen," I muttered.

Sawyer shot me an amused look. "Seriously? You've battled a zombie cyclops, decapitated a dead witch come back to life, and were almost killed by the Unseelie Queen, and *that's* the freakiest thing you've seen?"

"Oh, did I forget to mention today?" I brushed off some snow from the arms of my jacket. "That's the freakiest thing I've seen *today*. Who knows what tomorrow will bring?"

Rachel began to thrash weakly in his arms, and I smoothed my hand over her forehead.

"She's burning up." I eyed the gash on her head, wondering whether it had been caused by a fall or the rake of claws. I looked at Sawyer. "You don't think she's been infected, do you?"

He studied the bloody wound. "There's no way to tell yet. If she has, she's got a bigger battle ahead of her than just learning how to walk again."

Jesus. How in the hell was her mother going to take this news?

Hustling from the forest, we ran to the cabin. I gave a courtesy knock then opened the door, stepping aside to let Sawyer through. Lucy was standing in the small kitchen, a cup of what smelled like coffee in her hands. When she saw us, she dropped the cup. It shattered at her feet, black liquid creating a starburst around her shoes.

"Rachel?" she asked, voice shaking.

At Sawyer's nod, she rushed forward, coming to a stop a foot away, staring. She looked at my partner. "Is she... is she... *dead?*"

"No, but she needs medical attention."

"I'll call the ambulance," I told them, pulling out my phone.

"911, what's your emergency?"

"This is Officer McKenzie with Buxton PD. I need an ambulance at the Buxton Forest Lodge. I have a thirteen-year-old girl with a badly broken leg. She was also in the forest overnight, so I'm worried about exposure."

The sound of typing came over the line. "The road conditions aren't ideal for sending an ambulance, so I'll send in MediAir."

"How long will that take?"

"I can have them there in twenty minutes."

"Thank you."

When I returned to the cabin, Rachel was on the couch, her leg gently settled onto a cushion on the other end. Her mother was fretting over her, pushing back the hair from her forehead and talking in soft, gentle tones. My gaze finally found Sawyer's.

He held out a mug to me—a mug that had steam curling from the top.

I took a sip, closed my eyes, and enjoyed my transcendental moment. "Hello, caffeine. How I've missed you," I whispered.

Humor danced in Sawyer's eyes. "It's only been a few hours, pussy cat."

I glared at him over the rim of the mug as I took another sip. "Coffee to me is what sex is to you." Stroking the mug, I added, "I never want to be parted from you for that long again."

"Is the ambulance on its way?"

"They're sending a helicopter on account of the terrain. Twenty minutes."

He nodded and returned his gaze to Mrs. Hayes and Rachel. "What did you make of all that?"

"*All that* being the fact that a thirteen-year-old girl thought it was a good idea to go into the forest by herself while a savage werewolf was on the loose, or what did I make of the fact that we met and spoke to a tree? A tree, I might add, who was trying to help Rachel."

Humor danced in his gray eyes. "All of the above."

I took another draw from my cup. "Well, Sawyer, considering I've only been in this job since Thanksgiving, and we're now edging into New Year's territory, I'd say I'm handling it pretty great. No complete mental breaks. No postal moments."

"When's the ambulance coming?" Mrs. Hayes asked in a rough voice. I glanced over at the woman, finding her holding back tears as she stroked her daughter's hair.

"They're sending in a helicopter to get her. About fifteen more minutes."

She nodded and returned her eyes to Rachel. "Do you know who did this to her?"

A gash on the head and a broken leg didn't fit the same MO as the wolf we were chasing, but the dryad had confirmed it.

Just then, Rachel's eyes fluttered open—slowly—like it hurt to move that small part of her body.

"Rachel? Rachel, honey?" Lucy asked, sliding off the edge of the couch. "Are you okay?"

The girl moaned when she tried to move, tears beginning to streak down the side of her face.

Her mother stilled her movements. "Shh. I know you're hurting, baby, but help is on the way. Just rest now."

Rachel's bourbon-colored eyes found mine, and the intensity of her stare was unnerving.

Taking a knee beside the couch, I asked, "What is it?"

Her gaze flickered from her mother to me then back again. I nodded and patted her arm. Over my shoulder, I said, "Sawyer, can you please help Mrs. Hayes to gather some things for Rachel's trip to the hospital?" I hoped he'd take the hint and get Lucy out of there for a little while.

I let out a relieved breath when he said, "Sure. Mrs. Hayes, which bag should we use?"

Mrs. Hayes looked over at him, indecision clearly tearing her in two.

"I'll stay with her," I offered, giving her a smile. "This will help pass the time."

Although reluctant to leave her daughter, Lucy stood to delegate to Sawyer what to pack.

When we were alone, I leaned closer to Rachel and asked, "What is it?"

"I know who killed my brother," she whispered. "I tried to tell Mom, but she wouldn't listen. She didn't believe me."

This was it.

This was the break in the case we needed.

But I had to tread carefully. Rachel was still a minor, and her mother hadn't given her express permission to speak to her daughter about her involvement in our case. If I didn't ask her now, though, when else would I be able to?

I glanced over my shoulder then returned my attention to her. "What happened?"

"I saw Zach leave after dinner. He and Dad had been arguing about him not applying himself in college... not getting good grades. Zach left the cabin. I followed my brother outside and hid behind a log so he wouldn't see me. He didn't do very much, just smoke a cigarette and talked to his girlfriend on the phone. He got angry at something she said and started yelling. Then... then..." She swallowed. "I saw it."

I checked over my shoulder again. "Saw what?"

"The wolf."

Reaching into my pocket, I pulled out the crumpled-up drawing and smoothed it out. "The same one as you drew here? Black fur? Red eyes?"

"Yes."

I nodded. "How big was it?"

Her brow puckered for a moment. "At least the size of Jinx."

"Jinx?" I asked.

"My horse back home."

"What kind of horse is Jinx?"

"A thoroughbred. He's sixteen hands."

"So, it's a pretty big wolf?" I asked, just to check.

She nodded, then winced a little.

Glancing over my shoulder, I checked to see how much longer I had with her. "Why were you in the forest last night?"

She blinked her pretty bourbon eyes at me. "I wanted to find the wolf."

"Is that who attacked you?"

This time, she shook her head. "No. I was lost in the forest." She frowned. "It got foggy really quickly. I couldn't see anything in front of me. Then these balls of bright blue light appeared, and I followed them, but I wasn't watching where I was going. I tripped, and my foot got stuck." She looked down her body at her leg. "It hurts really bad. Is it broken?"

Placing my hand over hers, I replied, "We're going to get you help. The helicopter will be here any minute to take you to the hospital."

I could hear the rotors now, actually.

There was a knock on the cabin door.

"Officer McKenzie, there's a helicopter here," said Gregory in a tight voice. "It's landing in the parking lot. Do you know what that's—"

I shoved him out of the way, peered up at the sky, then stepped back inside. "Thanks, Greg."

"Gregory," he corrected.

I smiled, slammed the door, and walked back to Rachel. "Did you hear that? The helicopter is landing in the parking lot right about now to take you to the hospital."

"Where's my mom?" she asked.

"I'll get her."

I found Mrs. Hayes sitting at the end of Rachel's bed, her eyes fixed somewhere in the middle-distance while Sawyer packed a pink backpack with clothes from the drawers. He glanced over at me.

"She's going into shock, I think," he said, pulling the zipper across and placing the bag on the end of the bed.

Kneeling down, I touched Lucy's shoulder, hoping the connection would bring her out of her stupor. "Lucy, the helicopter has landed. The paramedics should be here…" I paused when I heard the knock on the cabin door. "Now. They're here now." Looking to Sawyer, I said, "Stay with her?"

"Of course."

Walking back out into the main living area of the cabin, I opened the door and smiled when I saw who it was.

"Berman. Jones."

"McKenzie?" Berman asked, a smile spreading on her lips.

"Well, if it isn't my two favorite paramedics." I let them in and showed them to the patient.

Berman immediately dropped her jump bag and started to triage Rachel's injuries. Jones, on the other hand, said, "What happened?"

"I swear, I had nothing to do with it this time. She was walking in the forest at night. It was foggy and…" I hesitated. Telling them Rachel was led down the garden path by balls of blue light seemed unnecessarily cruel. "And she tripped and fell over."

"How long was she out there before she was found?"

I did the mental math. "Maybe twelve to fourteen hours?"

"*Overnight?*" he asked incredulously. Jones's eyes flickered in Rachel's direction. "It had to be twenty degrees last night. Has she been given any drugs?"

"Not as far as I'm aware."

"Where are her parents?"

"Her mom is in the other room. I'll go and get her."

Leaving Berman and Jones to do their thing, I walked into Rachel's bedroom to find Lucy sobbing uncontrollably into her hands and Sawyer with an expression fixed somewhere between annoyed and compassionate.

I stifled my laugh, then, when I had myself under control again, I said, "The paramedics are here."

Lucy jerked her head up, blinked, then darted from the room.

"How's she taking things?" I asked, gesturing to the direction Lucy had run.

"Why did I have to be the one to do this?"

I frowned. "Do what?"

"Comfort her. You know I'm no good at that."

Actually, Sawyer was amazing with the comforting thing. It was just *who* he was comforting that made a difference. Hitching my hands onto my hips, I asked, "Are you saying I should've been here instead."

"It would make more sense."

"In what way?" I scoffed, walking to the window and looking out. "Because I'm a woman?"

"Because compassion is more hard-wired for you. I'm an incubus. All I know is sex."

Snorting this time, I retorted, "Yeah, you're right. Not a lot of compassion comes with seduct—" I yelped when Sawyer wrapped his arm around my middle and dragged me into the line of his body. His erection pressed against my lower back.

He growled into my ear, "You know that these verbal matches only turn me on."

"Anything turns you on," I replied, patting his hand and indicating I wanted him to let me go. We were on a case and *not* in private as he thought, despite our current isolation in Rachel's room. "You can show me just how bad of a girl I've been later. We have to get Rachel out of here and on that helicopter first. While you and Lucy were in here sharing a kumbaya moment, Rachel told me a little about what happened to her."

Sawyer immediately straightened. "What did she say?"

"She said she knew who attacked and killed her brother. She was there when it happened. Have you ever heard of electric blue balls of light appearing in the mist?"

Sawyer scrubbed a hand down his face. "Focus, pussy cat. *Who* attacked her brother?"

"She confirmed it was a big black wolf."

"Is that who attacked her last night? Because if it was, he's changing his MO. All Rachel suffered from was a broken leg and a knock to the head."

"No, it wasn't the wolf, although she had been looking for it. She said she'd gotten lost in the woods when she saw these balls of bright blue light that led her through the trees. She followed them."

He grunted. "Will-o'-the-wisps."

"Will-o'-the-*what?*"

"Will-o'-the-wisps. In Wales, my mother called them púca. They're incredibly small goblin-like fairies who lead people lost in the forest, or at night, toward something dangerous. Then they extinguish their lights and let that person struggle to find their way back."

"So, these will-o'-the-wisps are murderous?" And if they were, I needed to start making a compendium of all the things that wanted other things—namely *me*—dead.

It was going to be a looong book.

"Generally, no, but I have come across some that are."

"Well, *damn.*"

"Did Rachel say anything else?"

"That she broke her leg when her foot got stuck and she fell awkwardly." I studied his face for a moment.

"She was lucky she wasn't killed last night."

I nodded. Because, yeah, I didn't know how I'd feel having the blood of a barely teenage girl on my hands all because we hadn't found the wolf yet.

"McKenzie?" Berman asked from the doorway.

I spun around. "Yeah?"

"We've stabilized Rachel's injuries. We're going to get her and her mother loaded up on the bird. We're taking them to Buxton General."

Berman's eyes darted briefly to Sawyer then back to me. With one final nod and a wrap of her knuckles on the jamb, she disappeared.

Sawyer turned to me. "We need to return to where Rachel was found and take a look at the scene."

I shivered because who *actually* volunteered to go into a creepy forest with malicious mist and potentially murderous balls of light?

Oh, wait…

… that was me.

11

Sawyer and I returned to the reception area after the helicopter took off, and I hustled to the roaring fire in the hearth to warm my hands.

Gregory approached, concern etching lines around his eyes. "Is everything okay? Was Mrs. Hayes hurt?"

"Everything is fine, Greg," I replied, glancing around at the sound of hammering. I walked toward the section of wall on the other side of the foyer that had been newly taped off with plastic sheeting, and peered in. "What's going on?" I asked. "Expanding?"

"Yes," Gregory replied. "The lodge's dining room is getting extended and another six rooms are being added to each wing. The owner feels now is the time for the business to expand." His voice had gotten this faraway quality to it like he couldn't believe he was actually saying what he was. "Construction will begin in earnest in the new year."

"Huh." I would've thought it *wasn't* the time considering the bodies piling up and the complete lack of guests, but who was I to tell the guy how to run his business.

"Yes. Well. Was there something I could help you with?"

"Yeah, we need to search more of the areas surrounding the lodge. Are you able to provide us with a map of the lodge's walking trails and some walking poles? Maybe a daypack with some water and other supplies?"

"The recent snowfall will make it difficult to navigate. We have a snowmobile you can use. I'll have the concierge get everything together for you immediately."

I elbowed Sawyer. "You hear that? I get to drive a snowmobile!"

"Have you ever driven one before?"

Folding my arms, I gave him a sweet smile. "No, but you're going to let me drive one today."

He grunted. "Let's get gloves and evidence bags."

When we stepped back into the lodge's main building after retrieving what we needed from my truck, there was a rather chipper-looking man standing behind the concierge desk with a backpack resting on its surface.

"Detective Taylor? My name's Dale. Mr. Timmins said you needed some supplies?"

"Yes," Sawyer said. "Thanks for getting the provisions together so quickly."

He offered the keys to the snowmobile to Sawyer, but I yanked them out of my partner's hand before he could close his fist around them.

"Ha! Got them first."

Dale looked flustered, his gaze darting between us.

"It's fine," I told him. "Sawyer's legally blind, so I have to do the driving."

The concierge stared at Sawyer, obviously trying to figure out if that was true. He cleared his throat and handed me a day pack. "There's a map, compass, and some protein bars. I also put in some chemical hand warmers and a thermos of coffee."

Coffee? "Thanks, Dale!" I said, beaming. I shoved the pack at Sawyer's chest. "You're now my new favorite person."

The guy actually blushed. "Just doing my job, ma'am."

"Come on," Sawyer growled, shouldering the pack and turning toward the door.

"Ah, is he okay on his own?" Dale asked, gesturing to Sawyer. "I mean, does he need a cane or an assistance animal?"

I grinned even wider then chased after my partner. "If I didn't know any better, I'd say you were jealous," I sing-songed when I caught up with him.

He rounded on me. "Is that all it takes to win your affections? Coffee?"

"I'm a woman of simple tastes," I replied. "Coffee. Unicorns."

With a huff, he fed his other arm through the remaining strap on the pack. "And I'm legally blind now?"

"It was a tragic explosion at the marble factory," I told him sadly, shaking my head. "You were lucky to have escaped without any other injuries… other than your eyesight and your testicles."

He shook his head. "What the hell goes on inside your head?"

I shrugged. "Like I said, coffee and unicorns." I clapped excitedly when I saw the snowmobile that had been parked at the rear of the main building. It was completely black with a logo of the lodge painted in electric blue on the side.

I hopped onto it, sliding all the way forward and staking my claim as driver. Sawyer simply mounted the machine, settling in behind me. The heat of his body was instant, turning my low-simmering lust for him up to a full boil. Wrapping an arm around my middle, he pulled me backward into the front of his body—my shoulder blades pressing against his pecs.

I shivered.

He reached for the handlebars.

"Hey!" I tried to wriggle forward, but he held me tightly.

"You can't reach," he pointed out, whispering into my ear.

Dammit, he was right. I crossed my arms. "You did that on purpose."

His chuckle lit me up. "No, I'm just trying to keep my consort safe on this unpredictable vehicle."

"I'll have my revenge, Sawyer Taylor," I swore. "Just you wait. I hope you're not attached to your testicles."

"I thought I lost them in that marble factory accident," he replied. With his laugh still ringing in my ears, he twisted the throttle and sent us hurtling into the forest, following a walking trail that was clearly marked with wooden signs covered in snow. The wind whipped past my face, searing my skin. I scanned the forest as we moved through it, searching for anything that could give us a clue about the werewolf we were chasing.

About two miles away from the lodge, we climbed then crested a small hill, and the forest seemed to grow even thicker.

My opal gave a little throb of heat.

"My opal is reacting," I yelled over the whipping wind.

Ahead of us, the path suddenly stopped, making Sawyer ease off the throttle, slowing the snowmobile. He got off and walked to the fallen log, inspecting the base, finding it had snapped either during a storm or with a heavy snowfall.

"We have to go on foot from here."

I glanced around the forest. "Where is *from here*?"

"We're less than a quarter-mile from where we found Rachel," he replied, checking the map. "We've just gone around the other way. See? Come on."

He'd just helped me over the fallen log when I noticed some smallish footprints in the snow. Dropping onto my haunches, I touched the outer edge of the heel mark just as my phone started to ring.

"Officer McKenzie," I answered without looking at the screen.

"Well, hello, Officer McKenzie," Sasha said in a slow sexy drawl.

"What's up, Sash? Kind of working a case right now." I whistled to get Sawyer's attention. When he looked, I pointed at the print at the base of the holly bush.

"I'll be quick. You. Me. Wedding dress shopping. Tomorrow morning. You in?"

"Definitely."

"I'll send you the address. Meet you there at nine."

"Great."

"What have we got?" Sawyer asked, crouching down beside me.

Repocketing my phone, I replied, "A partial print."

"Looks small. A woman's maybe?"

"Yeah, I was thinking the same thing." But who else had come out this way, and when? All the guests had checked out.

"Let's keep moving."

We navigated through the forest carefully, dodging branches and roots that seemed to be reaching for us, to trip us up. I was listening to the sound of my breath whooshing in and out of my lungs when I heard chattering.

Tilting my head, I listened a little harder.

My opal pulsed, and the chatter started to make sense.

The forest god is merciful.

The forest god provides for us.

Someone's coming…

"Sawyer," I said quietly. "I don't want to alarm you, but we have some wood sprites nearby. I think they've found another body." Honestly, these creatures were better than cadaver dogs.

"Which direction, pussy cat?"

I tried to pinpoint where their voices were coming from then indicated directly ahead. "Up there."

Trying to be as quiet as we could, we walked toward the wood sprites, not really knowing what we were going to find. A dead body was a sure thing, but whose would it be, and what kind of state would it be in?

In the clearing, we found the wood sprites fluttering around the corpse.

A corpse I instantly recognized.

"It's Ms. Fraser," I told Sawyer, stepping closer to the wood sprites and waving them out of the way. "What the hell was she doing out here, and why hadn't she been reported missing?" I spotted Sage. "Sage, what the hell?"

The tiny wood sprite blinked up at me with her large emerald-green eyes—the complete picture of innocence. She began to talk in her dolphin-style speech, and my opal flared.

"What is she saying?"

"She's saying… *Wait*, slow down, Sage… She said the forest god has provided for them again."

"Who's their forest god? Can you ask them?" Sawyer tried to get a better look at the body. The members of Sage's harem swarmed closer to him when he tried.

"Who's your forest god?" I parroted. "Have you ever seen him? What does he look like?"

Chatter. Chatttttter. Chatter-chatter.

"Huh."

"What?" Sawyer said, inching a little closer.

"They said they've never seen him, just that they know he's a wolf. They've seen large paw prints around the forest where no man goes." I twisted around to face him. "It sounds like we just got another positive ID on the werewolf, but we still don't know who he is or where we can find him."

He dropped into a crouch just a few inches from the body and studied what was left of Ms. Fraser's perfectly painted face—not that there was much. Like before, the wolf had bitten most of it off, but the slash to the stomach and the throat were the same.

"Any teeth missing?" I asked.

He looked a little closer. "Yeah, like with Annabelle." He turned to me. "We need to find whoever he is soon, pussy cat, because we can't have this happening again."

"What the hell was she thinking coming out here alone?"

Chatter. Chattttter. Chatter-chatter. Chatter. Chatter-chatter.

"What?" I looked at Sage, who was perched on Betty's bent knee, her little legs folded under her body. "What did you say?" I listened. "She *came out here* looking for the forest god? When there's a crazy-ass plan to go into the heart of danger, I get called up for that job." I heaved a sigh. "Sawyer, we need to get the CSI team out here."

Nodding, he pulled the phone from his pocket and started dialing. I looked down at the wood sprites, who were still tearing pieces off Betty's corpse.

"Guys! Do you mind?" I listened to their chatter, then said to Sawyer, "Can you ask Lee to bring a steak with him? Apparently these three..." I gestured to Sage's harem with my thumb, "... can't go without a meal right now either."

12

After the elves had done their thing and Lee had taken Betty's body away, we returned to the lodge and told Gregory the bad news.

He sank into one of the leather couches in front of the fire, his cheeks draining of color and leaving his skin waxy. "I-I'm sorry. I don't…" His unfocused gaze found my face. "What did you say?"

"We found Betty's body out in the forest. She was attacked by the wolf we're looking for."

"What was she doing out there?" he asked in a barely-there whisper.

Sawyer and I shared a look. With the slight shake of his head, I knew he wanted me to keep my mouth shut. "We don't know," I said to Greg. "But I can assure you we're going to catch this killer."

Gregory stood suddenly, tugging at the bottom of his sweater. "I should let my employer know. I should tell him what's happened."

"Of course."

Just as quickly as he walked away, he ground to a halt and spun around to face us once more. "She has a brother... her only living family. You'll tell him?"

"Yes, we will."

He scrutinized my face for a moment. Nodded. Walked unsteadily through to the door that led into the back of house.

"We should go and notify her brother." Sawyer placed his hand on the small of my back and guided me to the front door. Snow fell in flurries around us as we made our way back to my truck.

I drove to the address we'd found listed for Betty's brother—David Fraser—pulling into the driveway. Shutting off the engine, I peered at the house that looked to be average in every single way.

"I hate this part of the job."

Sawyer grunted. "Sometimes it's harder than finding the bodies." He unbuckled his belt. "Come on. The sooner it's done, the sooner we can get home."

WHEN WE RETURNED HOME, ALL I WANTED TO DO WAS CURL UP IN BED, but Sawyer needed to feed. He took his time, despite how much exhaustion tugged at me. As my last orgasm in a long line of orgasms crested over me, I fell into a deep, blissful sleep, waking only when sunlight flooded through the window of my bedroom.

No, not *my* bedroom.

I was still in Sawyer's bed.

Wrapped in his arms.

Dammit, there went my rule to not stay in his bed.

He looked peaceful in sleep, his mouth curved into a small grin. His hairless bare chest rose and fell with his even breaths, his broad shoulders and muscular arms like a paradise for my tongue. The sheet draped across his waist was tented by an erection that made my mouth water. The longer I stared, the more violent the throb between my legs became. Jesus, his powers to seduce weren't even dulled when he was comatose.

Before I did something I regretted—namely hop on up and take a rough ride on his rock-hard shaft—I carefully extricated myself from his grip, being careful not to wake him. Padding back into my room, I stripped out of my panties and tank and took a much-needed shower. Stepping into the stall, hot water hit my still-sensitive skin, making me suck in a breathy moan. My whole body shivered with want, my brain flooding with memories of what Sawyer had done to me last night.

He'd taken me roughly the first time, like he was possessed with the need to *own* me before slowing things down to a torturous level, where he made me beg for it. I'd been more than happy to beg for it considering I wanted him as desperately as he wanted me. I didn't know what was going on, but the driving need to physically come together overtook us as soon as we had some privacy.

Sometimes not even when we had privacy.

Tilting my face up into the spray, I let the hot water sluice over me, then—out of habit—I looked down into the drain. I didn't want to have any grindylow or water pixie or whatever-the-fuck-would-scare-

Cat crawling out of there ever again.

Experiencing it once, it seemed, was enough for me.

Behind me, the shower door opened. Cold air swirled inside for a moment before Sawyer's whisky and chocolate scent wrapped around me.

He nuzzled my neck from behind, nipping the top of my spine gently. "You were quick to get out of bed this morning," he murmured into my ear, sucking on my earlobe and making me feel like I would melt into a delicious bliss puddle right at his feet.

I rubbed up against him like a cat in heat, groaning when his hard length brushed between my legs. "I'm meeting Sasha to go dress shopping, remember?" I panted.

He bit the side of my neck then sucked away the sting. "I remember, but my statement still stands." He drifted his hands down my shoulders, over my arms, and to my waist. With his fingers cinching shut, he pulled my ass more tightly into his hips. He was deliciously hard, and my aching body responded to his need, flooding with liquid fire.

Letting my head fall back against his shoulder, I let Sawyer work me with his magic hands, his nimble fingers finding the cleft between my thighs. I opened my legs a little wider, giving him better access to the very heart of me. We both groaned when he found my center.

"You're so slick. So *tight*," he growled.

"Shh, less talking," I mumbled, feeling an orgasm already cresting because when you banged an incubus, orgasms were a no-brainer, and they often came without any warning at all. "More... more..." I panted then shuddered as my pleasure crested without warning.

Sawyer dragged my lips to his, kissing me hard, thrusting his tongue inside my mouth. "More," he growled, positioning his hips so he could slide inside my body. I welcomed him in, taking the full length of him, breathing out a sigh of relief when he stayed there for a moment, letting me acclimate to his size.

"More," he said again, already moving inside me. All I could do was throw my hands out against the stall wall and widen my stance a little more. I wouldn't be getting a participation award for this session—Sawyer didn't need me to participate. All he wanted was my body, and I gladly gave it over to him.

Pleasure coursed through me, making every single one of my nerve endings sizzle and burn. His hands were everywhere. His mouth was *everywhere*, and still I needed more. More of him. More of how he made me feel—like I was cherished and loved and prized. More time to just enjoy him.

We came together, me screaming his name, him barking mine in a hoarse cry that echoed around the shower stall. He filled me up, and I felt every kick of his cock, sending me spinning into another orgasm that I was powerless to stop.

Black spots filled my vision as I let my head hang down, my arms still outstretched on the shower wall, barely taking any of my weight.

"Now, that's a good way to spend the morning," he said in a thoroughly worn voice behind me. Pulling out, he turned me around, kissed me then started to wash him away from my skin. I studied Sawyer as he worked, wondering why we had the connection we did. It was nothing to do with my opal, or who my family was. For the life of me, I couldn't see what he saw in me.

"Why are you staring at me?" he asked, keeping his eyes on my chest.

"Just wondering how I caught the attention of an incubus, held it, and became his consort."

"Yeah, I've been wondering that too," he said, completely serious for a moment before a huge grin spread across his lips.

I slugged him in the chest. "Seriously, though. Have you figured out anything else about this whole consort business?"

"Maybe." He frowned as he worked the loofah over my skin. "I spoke to someone who had once heard a story about an incubus who had a human consort."

"You did?"

"Hmm." He continued to clean me, paying particular attention between my legs.

I pushed him away, knowing what he was trying to do. "Well? What did they hear?"

With a sigh, he stopped his ministrations and looked at me. "He said he didn't know how it was possible, but the human stopped aging around the same time their consort bond was formed."

Bond? "Do *we* have a consort bond?"

He made a non-committal sound. "In a sense. In words, at least, but beyond that, I'm not sure it's enough."

"Can you find out what else we can do?"

He pushed his wet hair from his face. "Yes, I can." Leaning in, he kissed me slow and sweet. "I'd do anything for you, Cat."

I grinned. "Even go and make me some coffee so I don't have to wait around before leaving because you've officially made me late?"

"Yeah, even that." With one more kiss, he exited the shower, and I got to enjoy the utter perfection of Sawyer's naked body as he left the bathroom. He looked like he'd been carved from stone—bronzed, warm, hard stone. His pecs threw their own shadows, his abs a series of sixteen hard ridges down his torso. His broad shoulders gave way to muscular arms, a narrow waist, and muscled thighs and calves.

And I was one lucky woman to have him in my bed every day.

Turning off the water, I wrapped a towel around my breasts then rubbed another through my hair. When I got it as dry as I could, I stepped out then made my way to my walk-in closet. The racks were full now—a vast difference from what I had when I moved in a few weeks ago.

Sliding into a pair of jeans and a unicorn tee, I put on my motorcycle boots and tucked the warded cuffs into my back pocket. In my room, I checked out my burgeoning unicorn collection, smiling when I saw the overflowing shelves filled with new figurines and general unicorn paraphernalia. Even my bedspread had a unicorn on it, and I didn't care what people said—that bedspread was made in a king-size so that *clearly* meant it was also for adults.

The smell of freshly brewed coffee led me out into the kitchen, where I found Sawyer with just a towel wrapped around his hips as he worked the machine. I slipped onto one of the stools at the counter, rested an elbow on the granite, plonked my head in my hand, and watched him for a bit. When he turned around, a wicked smile graced his lips.

"Thinking about me naked?" he asked.

I shook my head. "Thinking about you making me coffee."

"I am doing that."

"I know. That's better than any other fantasy I could come up with."

"I should be offended."

I shrugged. "Probably."

With a shake of his head, he poured some coffee into my travel mug and placed it in front of me. "Have fun today. You deserve a day off but don't cause any trouble."

I swiped up my cup. "I think you meant to say, 'Don't get into trouble.'"

"Is there a difference?"

I took a sip of my coffee and sighed happily. "Of course, there is. One implies *I* started or looked for the trouble. The other that trouble came looking for me."

He made a see-sawing motion with his hand. "I stand by my original statement."

"You're such a dick," I told him, sliding off the stool. Grabbing my phone and keys, I shot him one last look over my shoulder. "What are you going to do without me here to entertain you?"

He laughed. "I've found a Keeper… one of the elves who keeps the records. I organized to meet them today." He checked the time. "In five minutes to be exact."

My heart thumped hard and loud in my chest. "Do you think you'll get an answer? About us?"

His broad shoulders rose and fell. "I don't know, but I have to try. I'll see you in a few hours."

I left the apartment, nursing my coffee in the elevator ride down to the parking garage. I got into my truck, stowing my precious cargo in the cup holder, then punching the address for the bridal shop into my phone's GPS since my new-old truck didn't have anything close to GPS as a feature.

I missed my old-new trucks.

With a sigh, I left the parking garage, and joined the early Sunday morning traffic. According to the GPS, I was heading across the river today, where boutique stores jacked up their prices by a bazillion percent, and everyone was happy about it. I couldn't blame Sasha for pulling out all the stops, though—she only planned on getting married once so she was doing it right. Plus, her fiancé and his family were loaded so why not take advantage of that?

I was taking a sip of my coffee when a Honda Civic coming in the opposite direction sped past, swerving into my lane as the driver checked over their shoulder. I hit the horn, disappointed when only a little squeak came out.

"Dammit. I hate this truck even more now!" After a second, I patted the worn dash. "I'm so sorry. I didn't mean that," I crooned. "You're the best damn make of truck around."

With my eyes on the rear-view mirror, I watched the driver of the Civic skid around the corner and disappear.

Man, there were some crazy people out today.

I refocused on the road that was steadily rising onto the bridge. More and more cars sped past in the opposite direction, the driver's terrified faces making my spider senses start to tingle. What was everyone driving *away* from?

I took another sip of coffee then slammed on the brakes as the driver in front of me yanked hard on the wheel and hung a sharp

Louie, the tires skidding and squealing as they hit the gas.

Rolling down the window, I yelled, "What the fuck is going on?"

The driver pointed frantically behind them before speeding off.

I frowned, turning to look.

Up.

Up.

Uppp.

"What the f—"

My heart slammed against my ribcage as I took in a huge spider web that weaved between the struts of the suspension bridge. The sticky silk threads were at least a foot thick and stretched for miles between the chunky steel cables. Around my neck, my opal flared with heat, the glow coming out from between the weave of my t-shirt.

I shook my head vehemently, my heart trying to leap out of my throat. "Nope. Na-uh. Not happening. I'm out."

Revving the engine, I jerked the wheel to the left, but the truck didn't move. I slammed my foot against the pedal repeatedly, the chassis wobbling with the torque the engine was throwing out but going absolutely nowhere. Suddenly, there was a metallic groan, and my truck tilted to one side, making me lean to the left. The belt across my chest cinched tight, and I pulled at the nylon sash trying to simultaneously save my life and break my ribs.

The next thing I knew, my head was spinning like I'd gone up a hundred floors in a high-speed elevator, while my stomach played catch up from waaay down on the ground. I peered out of my side window to see that, yup, I was hovering in the air—at least three hundred feet high. The vehicles that had been behind me were all turning around, heading in the opposite direction to the red and blue lights of the police coming my way.

Movement in the side mirror caught my attention, and it took me a moment to process what I was seeing. Swallowing my scream, I calmly picked up my phone which had miraculously stayed in the center console and dialed Sawyer.

"What did you forget?" he asked in an amused drawl.

"A giant can of Raid."

"What? Why? What's going on?"

"Well, you see, I was driving across the bridge, minding my own business—"

"Get to the point, McKenzie," he growled.

"Don't get snippy with me," I replied. "You know how I get when I'm scared."

"Extra babble-y."

I snorted. "Extra *amazing*. Anyway, the point is, there's a giant spider on the bridge, and I *may* have been caught in its web?"

"Why are you posing it like a question?" I could hear him grabbing his keys and slamming the door behind him. "Are you or aren't you in its web?"

"Why aren't you surprised or shocked by this development?" I asked, narrowing my eyes even though he couldn't see me.

He barked a humorless laugh. "Believe me, pussy cat, nothing about you surprises me anymore.

"Yeah, I'm in the web." I huffed, flicking my glowing necklace out of the way. Leaning forward, I looked out over the dashboard. Nothing by blue sky and birds. All things considered, this wasn't too bad. "But, hey, at least I'm still horizont—Gahhh!"

There was a loud *snap* that sounded a hell of a lot like high-tensile wire breaking. I yelped, dropping my phone and throwing my hands out to brace myself as my truck began to tilt forward. It clattered against the windshield, getting wedged between the glass and the dashboard.

"Cat? Sawyer barked in a panic-laced voice that I could still hear clearly. "Cat? McKenzie, answer me right now!"

Yelling, I said, "Jesus, I'm here! I dropped my phone."

"What the hell happened?"

"I'm dangling vertically in the air above the road."

He cursed, the sound of his motorcycle starting to drown out the juiciest combination of words I'd ever heard come out of his mouth. "I'm on my way."

The line went dead, and I hoped I wouldn't end up that way before he got here.

Twisting around in my seat, I tried to look out the rear window of the cab, and immediately regretted it.

The giant spider was still there, but all I could see was its clicking jaws and palpitating front legs. It felt the way along the side the truck, the *tap, tap, tapping* along the steel frame setting my teeth on edge. After an investigation that seemed to last an eternity, the spider disappeared from view. My relief was short-lived when my truck began to spin—slowly at first—but then steadily increased in speed.

On the next revolution, something clunked me in the back of the head. Reaver had dropped from the back seat, landing into the footwell on the passenger side. I tried to reach for it, but with the tension on my seat belt keeping me in place, I had nowhere else to go. Throwing out my hands—one on the window and one on the wheel—I tried to keep my equilibrium.

I lost that one so hard.

In no time at all, I was dizzy and nauseous and…

… going blind?

No, not blind.

The cab of my truck was getting darker and darker until the only source of light was the blue glow from my opal dangling in front of my nose.

I reached for the window crank, having to use more muscle to get it open than I thought I would. Cold air flooded in, making me wish I'd bothered to put on a sweater instead of just a t-shirt this morning. Then again if my truck was dropped from three hundred feet, whether or not I opted for warmer clothing would be a moot point.

How am I supposed to get out of this one? "Think, McKenzie, *think!* You fought off Baba Yaga when she was alive *and* dead, a zombie cyclops, kappas, and vampires. You can get out of this one too."

My gaze landed on Reaver.

Straining, I reached for the sword again, feeling the edge of the nylon belt cutting in. The truck was still spinning, reminding me of the burrito lunch van guy rolling up my lunch.

Wait…

Was that what was happening?

Reaching through the open window, I touched the barrier that surrounded my car. It was tacky to the touch, and I immediately knew what it was.

Spider silk.

I was being spun.

Like a fly that was caught for lunch.

With the knowledge that the spider was going to inject me with poison to liquify my insides in order to suck them right out again, my efforts to reach Reaver became more desperate. But every time my fingertips brushed against the hilt with one revolution, I was frustratingly torn away from it in the next.

My head throbbed in time with my erratic pulse, the sound of my panicked breaths my only company.

Then as quickly as the spinning had started, the truck returned to horizontal once more. I groaned in relief as all the blood in my body stopped rushing to my head and returned to my extremities. Outside my open window, I heard the wail of police sirens and the screams of onlookers.

Was Sawyer out there now?

Was he seeing this?

My phone rang, and I leaned forward to grab it as it slid from the dash. I glanced at the screen before answering, "Sash, now isn't really a good time."

"Girl, tell me about it. I'm going to be late. I'm stuck trying to get across the bridge, but there's a freaky-ass giant spider and its web across the suspension wires. Have you and lover-boy been called to the scene?"

"We're both here," I replied, trying to sound less terrified than I felt. I didn't want to stress out the bride-to-be. "So, I guess this means

I won't be able to make it to the dress-shopping expedition."

"Why not? The spider is moving away now."

I pulled my phone away from my ear when there was a beep. Sawyer was calling me. "Argh, Sash, I have to go. I'll call you later, okay?"

"Yeah, yeah. I'll speak to you then."

She hung up, and I answered Sawyer's call.

"Why the hell did you take so long to answer?" he barked.

"Hey, don't be mad at me. Sasha called."

"Did she also tell you, you were being carried away by a giant spider?"

"Yeah, she did mention that." I flicked a crusty, old Band-Aid from the knee of my jeans. "Man, I need to get this truck properly cleaned. There are still ghosts from its previous owner lurking around in here."

"Can you focus?" he hissed.

He *wanted* me to focus on the fact that I was terrified and being carried away by a giant spider? "I am focused. Although to be fair, there's not much to focus on in here other than all the horrible ways I could die."

"You are not going to die." His voice was laced with determination. "You're *not* going to die."

"Yeah, well, from where I'm sitting, it feels like I am. Where in the hell is this spider taking me anyway?"

"I'm hopping on my motorcycle right now. I'm going to follow you."

"Couldn't be too hard, right? It's a giant spider the size of... the size of... say, how big is it?"

"At least the size of a shipping container."

Yeah, that didn't help with the panic levels.

"Don't let it out of your sight," I whispered.

"I won't. I'll see you soon, okay?"

I nodded, even though he couldn't see me. I had to stay strong. If I flipped out and broke down now, things wouldn't get any easier.

"I have to hang up for a minute so I can get on my motorcycle," Sawyer told me calmly. "I'll call you back as soon as I can."

I gripped the door rail until my knuckles were white. "Okay."

The line went dead, and I let out a breath. I guess all I could do was wait. Glancing down, I saw my travel mug was still there, upright, and without a drop spilled.

Things were looking up.

13

"Four thousand, three hundred and fifty-five Mississippi. Four thousand, three hundred and fifty-six Mississippi. Four thousand, three hundred and fifty-seven Mississi—"

The gentle rocking I'd become accustomed to suddenly stopped. No more Mississippis could be counted, but I guess it didn't matter. Counting Mississippiously wasn't an accurate way to measure time *or* distance, no matter how much I wanted it to be.

It was a great distraction, though.

I was jostled in my seat as my truck was dropped back to the ground, my head hitting the roof.

"Owww!" I complained even though nobody was there to listen to me. I rubbed the crown of my head to take away the sting. Putting my now empty travel mug back into the cup holder, I unclipped my seat belt and leaned over the center console to gather Reaver from the footwell, but the sword had once more disappeared without me noticing.

I didn't know whether to take that as a good sign or not. Reaver did have the tendency to show up when I most needed it, and call me crazy, but being wrapped up as a tasty spider burrito and being carried halfway across the city in my truck *kind of* seemed like the time I most needed it.

I straightened, looking around at the interior of my truck bathing in the blue glow of my opal, noticing the color was weakening. Turning around, I saw that there were slashes in the web—holes that were letting in the... moonlight?

Through the gaps, I caught glimpses of a man with high cheekbones, caramel skin, dark eyes, and pin-straight long black hair. He was dressed in old, ripped jeans and a flannelette shirt over a gray Henley.

It was the guy from the tape—from Annabelle's murder.

"Stay calm, McKenzie," I muttered under my breath. "You're only unarmed and coming face-to-face with a murderer. No biggie."

I tracked his progress around the truck as he slashed and hacked his way through the spider silk. When the passenger side window was clear, he opened the door—the hinges creaking ominously just like in a B-grade slasher flick. I scooted back against my door, pressing my spine closer to the molded plastic trim.

"Don't come any closer," I said, grabbing my travel mug and brandishing it at him. Dammit! Why couldn't I have left some scalding hot liquid in there to throw in his face? "Stay where you are."

A frown marred his otherwise perfect skin. "Excuse me?"

"I said stay where you are."

"I'm just trying to help you."

My gaze flickered down to the opal. It wasn't glowing… yet. "I have help coming."

At my statement, his brows rose. "You do?" He made a show of looking around. "We're in the middle of the forest. How do you suppose they'll find you?"

"He'll find me."

"Well, how about you come and warm up in my cabin while you wait?"

I shook my head, loose tendrils of my teal hair slapping my cheeks. "No. I'm staying here."

The man's eyes flashed with impatience before he grinned at me, revealing straight, white teeth. "I'm not going to hurt you. Just come out of the truck."

"Yeah? I'm pretty sure that's what every serial killer says before they hack their victims to pieces."

He put his gloved hands up in front of him like he was surrendering. "Suit yourself, but that spider will be back. She never goes far when her dinner is waiting."

He stepped away from the door and disappeared from view. I waited a few moments before sliding across the seat and peering out. He was right about one thing. We were in the forest, but I had no idea *where* in the forest I was. The wind whipped through the trees, making the branches creak and the leaves rustle. I peered up into the midnight-dark sky, seeing the bright, twinkling stars.

Jesus, how long had that spider carried me?

Lowering myself to the ground, I edged around to the front of my truck and let out a breath when I got a proper look at the damage. The entire body was wrapped up solid in spider silk, reminding me of a bug that had been trapped in a web.

A twig snapped somewhere behind me, and I spun around, my gaze scanning the trees.

"You're just being paranoid, McKenzie," I chided quietly. "You're being jumpy because you're unarmed, the werewolf is out there, you have no idea where you are, and you're out of coffee."

The wind wound through the bare trees, the noise they made like a banshee's wail—well, what I *assumed* a banshee's wail would sound like. I hadn't actually ever met one before. The wind brought with it the scent of woodsmoke, and a whole-body shiver racked me. I didn't want to confront the killer—I was surprised he'd actually *left* me unharmed when he found me—but if I could find where he was staying, it would be easier to come and arrest him afterward.

"You'll be unable to find him on your own," a softly melodic voice said. I turned my head to find the dryad standing a few feet away. She was still wearing the bark bustier, the Spanish moss in her antlers swaying ever so slightly in the breeze. "He is, however, the monster you seek. But he is far more powerful than you give him credit."

"He's the werewolf?"

"No." She stepped closer, folding her hands together in front of her. "He is the Amaroq."

Amaroq? "I've not heard of an amaroq before." I tapped my chin. "Unless you count the truck? That's spelled with a 'k' though. Is this amaroq spelled with a 'k'?"

"There is only one Amaroq. He is legend among the Inuit people of these lands. The wood sprites call him a god. I call him a butcher."

I started to lean against the front of my truck, remembered it was covered in spider silk, and folded my arms instead, huddling against the cold. "Why is he killing these people?"

"He was woken from his hibernation by a number of snowmobilers on the forest trails. Then by the construction noise from the lodge. This… angered him."

"That's putting it mildly." If this was him angered, I didn't want to see him in an all-out rage. "The victims were killed by a wolf, though, *not* a human being." Or had we been blind and not seen something else on the victims that would've told us that?

"He can shift into a wolf at will. He moves like water, his form changing between one breath and—"

A howl tore through the night air.

The dryad's expression shifted to fear—my stomach twisting into a knot too. She tugged at my bare arm, her fingers cold and hard like a piece of solid timber wrapped around my bicep. "Quickly. You must move quickly. *Now*," she urged. "This way."

Another howl—this one closer than before.

With the dryad's arm still wrapped around my arm, she pulled me through the forest while my opal bounced on the outside of my shirt. It illuminated the jagged branches, and overgrown path in front of my feet…

… it also illuminated the thousands of spiders racing through the forest alongside us.

Were they fleeing the Amaroq too?

I risked a glance over my shoulder then wished I hadn't. The forest was alive with the little beasts, covering the trunks of trees and ground in a living, writhing blanket.

"Spiders," I gasped, my throat raw and my lungs burning. "Why are there so many spiders?"

"Anansi," the dryad said without looking at me.

What was Anansi? My foot got stuck on an exposed tree root, and I crashed to my knees. Letting out a small cry, I was waiting for the throbbing to stop when the dryad slid her hand under my arm and lifted me.

"You must keep going." Pointing ahead, she said, "See the pocket of sun? Run for it. Don't look back. I'll try to buy you some time."

"Time? Time for what?"

"The Amaroq can only move around under the moon's glow." She turned me around, shoving me in the back. "Now, go!"

I took a few steps away then glanced back at her, my heart a loud thump in my chest. "What about you?"

"Don't worry about me. Go!"

With my knees still protesting, I clambered over the snowy ground, careful to avoid the tree roots I could see. Behind me, another howl pierced the cold night air, and my opal flared more brightly.

Up ahead, there was a clear demarcation between night and day, and it was only fifty feet away now.

Thirty.

Twenty.

Ten.

A blood-curdling scream made me stop a foot away from safety. Turning—breathless—I scanned the trees. The spiders had stopped their pursuit of me, stalling out fifteen feet away, but that wasn't what drew my attention. It was the growls and snarls that echoed through the trees, the sound of an unseen battle wrapping around me. I had to help her. I had to...

Something hard gripped my arm, yanking me backward.

I swallowed back the scream when I saw it was Sawyer.

Sunlight flooded my retinas as he pulled me out of the night and into the bright midday sun. Gripping my biceps tightly, he ran his gray eyes all over me.

Panting, I tried to shove him away. "We have to help her."

"Who?"

"*The dryad.*"

Twisting, I freed myself of his grip and dashed back into the night. The air was instantly colder, seizing in my lungs. I strained my ears, trying to pinpoint where the fight had moved to, but there was nothing but an eerie quietness to the place that made the fine hairs on my arms stand on end.

Running forward, I tumbled over a tree root and fell to my hands and knees. Sawyer was there, though, hauling me up. I took off again, skidding to a stop when I reached a spot in the trees that looked like it had been splashed with amber liquid.

Sawyer, who had drawn his Glock at some point, crouched down and touched the pools of sticky... sap?

"It's the dryad's blood."

"Where is she?" I looked around, taking a few steps forward. Movement from the corner of my eye caught my attention. *There!*

"Sawyer."

Falling to my knees, I took the dying dryad's hand in mine and squeezed gently. From the bottom of her ribcage down, there was nothing left—only dangling roots dripping in more of that sap.

Her eyes fluttered open weakly. When she focused on my face, she rasped, "Go."

"We can get you help." Even as I said the words, I knew it was bullshit. There would be no way to help her. Instead, I smoothed back the hair from her forehead. One of her antlers had been broken in the fight, more of that amber liquid leaking from the end.

"You... saved my life."

Her eyes closed, her chest rising and falling slowly. "Now... you have to... free her," she muttered. "Free her... from him."

"Who?" When she didn't open her eyes again, I squeezed a little harder. "Free *who?*"

"Cat," Sawyer said.

Meeting his gaze, I swiped away the tears that dribbled down my cheek. I looked back at the dryad, hoping to ask her more questions, but she was already gone. Her body was *gone*. Frantically, I scanned the forest around me. "Where is she?"

"Her body returned to the earth."

Fisting my hand tightly, I released it and stood, brushing the snow and dirt from my knees. I ignored the fresh wave of tears still trying to spill down my face.

"I'm sorry, pussy cat."

I shrugged, trying to play it totally cool. "It's fine. I mean, it sucks that she had to die." Especially while trying to save *my* life. Squaring my shoulders, I met his gaze. "Who is it that she wants me to help?"

"I don't know. But we should start with things we do know. Where did the spider take you?"

"It dropped me in a clearing not too far from here."

"Do you remember where?" He began studying the ground, looking for any signs that I'd come this way before.

"No, but it was in the middle of a forest where every tree looks the damn same. Finding where I was dropped is like trying to find a needle in a haystack. Worse! It's like trying to find a generation alpha without a social media addic—"

"I found your tracks," Sawyer said matter-of-factly. He pointed to the north. "You came from that direction."

He started forward, leaving me to follow or get left behind.

Given my propensity for getting into trouble, I followed.

Eventually, we came to the clearing where my truck had died.

Sawyer approached my trashed vehicle, touching the spider silk covering every square inch of the hood. "How did you get out of there?"

Peering inside the cab, I said, "The Amaroq freed me... Damn, still no Reaver." I stepped backward, slamming into Sawyer's chest. "Jesus, Sawyer. Give a girl a little warning," I whined, rubbing at my arms to ward off the spark of awareness that was running all over my body now that he was so close again.

"The Amaroq?" His question came out in a cold, calm voice. "You didn't mention the Amaroq before."

"Yes, well, I'm mentioning him now. That's who's been murdering the campers and the guests at the lodge. He went to the cabin with the express purpose to kill Annabelle."

"Aside from this, it's the first time you've mentioned it…" he started. I gave him the stink eye. "The Amaroq is just an Inuit legend."

"Yeah, well, I met him. I can tell you he's very much *not* just an Inuit legend."

I moved around to the side of my truck, bending down to look at the damage the spider's legs had made to the bodywork.

"What did he say to you?"

"He totally played it cool. Said I could wait for you in his cabin. Said I'd be safe. After he left, the dryad found me and helped me get out of this seemingly perpetual nightmare."

"That's it? He didn't try to harm you *at all*?"

"Look, I know I'm not everyone's favorite person, but no, he didn't try to harm me. He just tried to lure me away." I walked to the edge of the clearing and scanned the trees, looking for the little spiders that had joined me on the impromptu fun run through the forest. "Do you think the spider will come back to finish off the job?"

"I don't think she ever intended to kill you, pussycat," he replied, coming to stand beside me. "If she had, she would've done it at the bridge. Why carry you miles away to just leave you in the truck?"

"I wasn't trying to think about it."

"Well, maybe you should."

Nope! Not even willing to entertain that one. My gaze landed on yet another one of my destroyed trucks. "What are we going to do about my truck? We can't leave it here, can we?"

I'd already left one in Wonderland. I didn't want to become known as that cop who didn't clean up after herself.

Sawyer looked around. "The forest is too dense to get a tow truck in here. For now, we'll have to leave it."

When we finally found our way back through the forest, the path we were on spat us out on one of the trails the lodge guests used. Only the main building's lights were on, and as we walked through the doors, we found out why. Gregory was behind the reception desk, but the lobby itself was empty. He looked up when we approached, his expression somber.

"Detective Taylor, Officer McKenzie, I didn't realize you were on the premises."

"Unrelated body-snatching incident," I said. "*My* body this time. And a gigantic spider."

Color leeched from the manager's cheeks. "A s-s-spider?"

Hiking my thumb in the direction of the woods, I replied, "Living back there somewhere."

Gregory pulled a crisp white handkerchief from his pocket and blotted the sweat from his brow. "Oh. Oh… I see." His eyes darted to Sawyer. "Do you have any more information about Betty's…" His words petered out like he couldn't bring himself to actually say *death*.

"Not yet," Sawyer assured him. "But we're getting closer to cracking this case."

"Why does this place look like a ghost town?" I asked.

Gregory's skin turned waxy. "After the unfortunate deaths of Ms. Peters and Ms. Fraser, and the injury sustained by the young Ms. Hayes, the owners of the lodge have decided to close for the foreseeable future. Bookings were non-existent in any case, and Mrs. Hayes has checked out to be closer to her daughter in town." He heaved a sigh. "I think the timing is advantageous, though. It will give the construction crews free rein on the property to complete the expansion and refurbishment."

"Yeah, about that…" I started.

"Yes?"

"The construction is the reason your guests are getting attacked."

I felt Sawyer's cool gray eyes slide to my face. *Shit, I'd forgotten to tell him I knew that, didn't I?* I'd blame that on being scared. Glancing over my shoulder at him, I shrugged—*I'll explain later.*

Gregory gaped. "I beg your pardon?"

"All these attacks are linked to the lodge." Well, except for those two brothers. That attack seemed unrelated.

"I don't u-understand," Gregory stammered, looking to Sawyer for clarification.

But Sawyer kept his gaze locked on me, giving me the reins of his conversation.

"We've been told that the attacks are happening because the perpetrator is unhappy about the construction noise on the mountain."

"Well, he could've lodged that complaint before work began," Gregory blustered. "There was more than enough time to voice their disagreements at the council meetings we'd held. Not to mention the numerous notifications we posted online and in the newspaper. Nobody else disagreed with the proposal to expand."

"I guess the guy didn't get the memo," I reasoned. "In any case, this is what's happened, so how likely is it that the construction can stop at least for a little while until we apprehend him?"

"Mr. Scali and his partner have been wanting to expand for over a decade," Gregory said.

Mr. *Scali*? Turning to Sawyer, I said, "We need to return to the office."

His brows rose in question.

Me, volunteering to working on a Sunday? If it meant catching this killer? You betcha.

"Greg," I added, turning back to the manager. "Can I suggest you relay this information to your boss, and you get out of here until we catch this killer?"

14

"Scali," I said to Sawyer after I dismounted his bike at the precinct, flexing out my fingers from the kung-fu grip I'd had on his body. It had started snowing on our way back into the city, making the city roads more treacherous than usual.

"What?"

"Scali," I repeated. "The two young men we first investigated were also named Scali. What are the chances that we're dealing with the same family?"

"Too much of a coincidence," he replied, brushing the snow off my shoulder. "Once we confirm it, we can start digging a little deeper into the history of the lodge and see what else we can find out."

I nodded. "Let's get inside before we freeze to death."

The bullpen was empty except for a couple of beat cops who had come in from the cold to warm up and get coffee. The PIG offices were also empty.

Rounding my desk, I asked, "Where do you want to start?"

"General research into the lodge's history then missing persons. That may give us enough to try and tie this all together."

"You take missing persons. I'll do general history." Turning on my computer, I spun around in my chair while I waited for it to boot up. On my next revolution, I saw my home screen wallpaper and drew myself to a stop. Opening a browser, I started with the easiest search term—Buxton Forest Lodge.

I clicked into the first site, which was from the official website. The Buxton Forest Lodge had been constructed thirty-five years ago. The actual build had started off without incident, but about a month after construction started, workers were disappearing from the site. Missing Person Reports had been lodged with the police, but their bodies had never been found.

"Greene Construction was the company they used to build the lodge originally," I told Sawyer, flicking through a newspaper article. "Ground-breaking was in May and they finished in…" I scrolled down. "Damn! Like seven years later. Why would it take so long?"

"If they kept losing construction workers, that would explain the long build time."

"You were on the Force back then, right?" Sawyer had been a cop for decades already even though he only looked to be twenty-five. Being an incubus, and before the time of the Reveal, he'd had to keep his head down even if he suspected supernatural involvement in a crime.

"I was but not in Buxton. I never heard anything about this. If I had, I would've come to investigate it myself."

Leaning back in my chair, I folded my hands over my middle. "So, these guys died, and nobody knew why or where their bodies were, and *nobody* thought to investigate it?"

"They were isolated on top of a mountain. There was only one place for them to go and that was the forest, and as you've seen first-hand, the forest is a confusing place."

"Yeah, especially if the Amaroq did that weird night-time trick."

Sawyer said, "He must use it to confuse his prey, put them off balance so he can attack more easily."

"If I were a shape-shifting, Inuit legend, that's how I'd do it."

Sawyer stared at me.

"What? I said *if*." I brushed some lint from my jeans. "Anyway, that's not the reason he creates the night. The dryad told me he could only move around under the light of the moon."

Sawyer said, "According to legend, the Amaroq stalked hunters who were stupid enough to move around at night."

"What I really want to know is where he stashed the bodies of those men from thirty-five years ago?"

"I don't know, but if we find them, we can close this cold case and give a lot of families closure."

"We need to find out where the Amaroq is holed up."

Sawyer arched a brow. "You actually *want* to go find him now?"

"I never miss an opportunity to be worshiped like a god."

"You get worshiped every day in my bed." His cool gray eyes darkened suddenly, and I felt his need rise. It was as if the air itself was pumped full of pheromones, and both Sawyer and I were powerless against them.

"Do you need to feed?" I asked in a hoarse whisper, my whole body warming at the idea. I stifled a moan when my lower body clenched in anticipation. The thought of having sex with Sawyer right now was all-consuming, even if it was completely inappropriate to do this at work. I always thought we had boundaries, but when he looked at me like that, I'd happily throw a match on my standards and watch them burn.

Maybe pour a little gasoline on top just for good measure.

"We can go home if you want?"

A wicked grin formed on his face, and when he spoke, his voice was husky. "Who says we need to go home?"

I looked around our office, whispering, "Here?"

"No, not here. There's a janitor's closet near the weapons room."

"You want to take me to a janitor's closet?" *Was he serious?* And why was I stalling on this one? I stood. "Where is the damn thing?"

Taking me by the hand, he led me out of the office and down the short hallway toward our weapons store. There was only one other door and Sawyer twisted the knob on it so hard that the bolt and locking mechanism snapped.

With a snarl, he shoved the door out of our way and shut it behind us.

"How are we going to—"

My words were stolen when he pushed me against the door and covered me with his body.

His hands were everywhere, seeking, touching, stroking.

His mouth was everywhere, licking, tasting, savoring.

I opened for him, a moan escaping me.

I'd seen Sawyer desperate before, but he'd also been restrained—holding himself back in case he hurt me.

Today was different. For some reason he was almost frantic in his need to touch, to claim.

"I'm sorry," he growled into my ear, nipping the lobe.

"Why? I'm not." No, I wasn't sorry he was losing control here. I think I needed it just as much as he did after my spider adventure today. I gasped when he burrowed his hands under my shirt, cupping my breasts roughly and thumbing my nipples.

My first orgasm crested on a beautiful wave which I rode for as long as I could.

Sawyer purred his approval, lowering to his knees in front of me. With an easy flick of his wrist, he undid the button on my jeans and pulled down the zipper. I was stepping out of them a moment later, blinking at where my boots lay haphazardly around the room.

Damn, the male was good. I didn't even realize he'd taken them off me.

Without preamble, his mouth was between my thighs, his tongue darting out to taste me. Slamming my hands back against the wall, I held on for the ride of my life. With exquisite, torturous strokes, he teased me into submission, coaxing not one but two orgasms from me.

With each moan, with each groan, with each time I grabbed his hair and held him closer, he became more desperate until finally, he stood.

His eyes were the darkest black, swirling pools of unslaked lust. Without losing eye contact, I undid his belt and jeans, freeing his hard cock. My gaze drifted lower because, how could I *not* look at him? He was a magnificent lover with an utterly amazing dick.

When my eyes returned to his face, strain branched from the lines around his sinful mouth. He looked as if he was in pain.

"What's wrong?" I whispered into our quiet, secret space.

"I feel like…" He shook his head, fisting his hands at his side. "I feel out of control, and I don't want to hurt you."

"You won't." I uncurled each of his fists and placed his hands on my waist. "You won't hurt me."

I felt his indecision snap like a rubber band. One minute, he was standing in front of me. The next, he was inside me.

Claiming me.

With each thrust of his hips, he stroked deeper and deeper. The air was charged with something more than lust. There was an undeniable *need* between us. One to claim and the other to *be* claimed. It felt like desperation, but what we were desperate for besides each other, I wasn't sure.

Sawyer's next thrust inside me was so deep I gasped, the sound breaking through the sexual haze and causing him to stop.

"Are you okay?"

"Yes. Feels good… just different."

"I know," he moaned. "It feels… urgent."

Urgent. Yes, that's what it was. Like we had to strip each other's clothes off as soon as possible. To be skin-to-skin. To claim.

"Do you think we've been bespelled again?" I wondered out loud, moaning as the first signs of another orgasm blinked into existence. That had to be the reason we were so savage with each other.

Sawyer shook his head. "Your opal." Thrust. "Not." Thrust. "Glowing." Thrust.

He was right. Beneath my shirt, my opal was only warm because of my flushed skin. I opened my mouth to ask him another question when my orgasm slammed into me.

Thrusting my head back, I absorbed every sensation, every nuance of it. This orgasm felt like no other—stronger, more potent, perhaps. But why? Why would it feel like—

My thoughts turned to mush when I realized Sawyer had sunk his teeth into the flesh between my neck and shoulder. I didn't jerk away—not that I could even if I wanted to. Sawyer held me still with his teeth, but the rest of his body was still in the game. He pumped harder, held tighter, groaned louder.

Driven by deep instinct, because I would *never* have allowed anyone to bite me, I rested my hand on the back of his head, feeling the silken lengths of his hair against my palm. I pushed his head closer, drawing in a surprised breath when I heard gentle suckling. I was trying to bring myself to care that he was using me like a juice box, but like everything with Sawyer, I embraced it.

He tore his mouth from my shoulder, a trickle of blood coasting slowly from the corner of his mouth, and roared as he released into me. His orgasm triggered another for me, and together we fell down the rabbit hole of pleasure edged with razor-sharp thorns of pain.

As I breathed through the aftershocks that were zipping through my body like faulty fireworks, I wondered again whether we had been bespelled. Sex with Sawyer was always ah-mazing, but what we just did? It seemed like someone else had been driving our passions.

"Oh, fuck, pussy cat, did I hurt you?" He touched the side of my neck where his teeth had been buried just a few moments before.

"No. It didn't hurt." I thumbed back his upper lip, expecting to find fangs there. Succubi—the incubi female equivalent—had fangs, but as far as I knew, incubi didn't. "I thought you didn't do that like succubi did."

He clasped my hand gently and turned it over so my palm faced him. Placing a gentle kiss there, he lowered it to my side. "We don't." He frowned and shook his head. "I've never heard of this happening before." His tormented gaze returned to my savaged neck. "I don't know what came over me. I just felt like there was someone inside my head pushing me to mark you, to take your blood."

"If this had happened a couple of weeks ago, I would've been in freak-out territory right now, but I know I can trust you. I *do* trust you."

He shook his head, his expression still stricken. "I'm so sorry." Sliding from my body, he kissed me on the mouth and said, "Let's get you cleaned up."

15

"Thanks, Jen," I said, picking up my coffee order in my unicorn travel mug. Sawyer reached for his, flashing a smile at Jen that would surely set the girl swooning.

Annnd there was the swoon. Jen had to prop herself up on the counter to stop herself from melting into a puddle at Sawyer's feet.

"Are you okay, Jen?" I asked.

She mopped her brow, her eyes still on Sawyer. "I'm great. Fantastic, even. Never better."

I turned away, dragging my stupid-hot partner with me. "You should only use your powers for good," I told him, taking a draw from the top of the cup.

"That was good." He smirked, but his easy expression didn't last. His gaze flickered down to where a white bandage under my shirt covered the bite he'd given me yesterday in the janitor's closet. Guilt was eating him up, and no matter how many times I told him it was okay, I knew he was struggling to come to terms with this.

I glanced up when I felt someone staring at me. A young woman stood in the line, waiting to order, her unhuman gold eyes with acid-green striations pinned on me. She was dressed like a character from *Sailor Moon*—all high school prep girl meets sex siren. The only thing that didn't fit with the costume was the solid gold band around her throat rather than the red choker Sailor Moon favored.

"Leopard shifter," Sawyer said quietly into my ear, steering me away by the elbow. "And a slave to another supe."

I turned to gawk at him. "I'm sorry, what did you say? Slave?"

He nodded, grim. "Your society may have abolished slavery hundreds of years ago, but the supernatural world still plays by its own rules."

I glanced back over my shoulder, trying to catch another glimpse of the girl. "How do you know she's a slave?"

"The gold band around her neck."

My blood boiled at the injustice. "*Who* does she belong to?" Because I was going to go and kick their ass.

"It doesn't matter who she belongs to. You can't do anything about it. For supes, keeping a slave isn't about legalities. It's about punishment, ownership, entitlement, or recompense. Sometimes all four."

"This is the first I've heard of it."

Sawyer pushed open the door for me, his hand hot on my lower back. "You have to remember that most of us aren't civilized by your standards."

"Believe me, I'm starting to see that." I took another sip of my coffee, squeezing past the line of cops waiting to get their injection of morning wake-me-the-fuck-up. Since the coffee shop was just around the corner from work, a lot of cops stopped in there on the way into the precinct. With me hanging around with a detective now, coffee and I had formed a symbiotic relationship. Well, even *more* of a symbiotic relationship.

"I knew you'd sleep with at least one of them, supe whore," someone sneered as we stepped away from the line of people.

I looked up to find Smith standing there with one of his buddies—a beat cop named Daye. "Supe whore? If you wanted maximum impact on an insult, always go with alliteration. Now, supe *slut* would've worked so much better. Supe *strumpet* might also be okay, but only if we were living in the 1800s. And who I sleep with isn't your concern, Smith."

He scowled and took a step toward me. "You'll get yours one day, McKenzie."

"I hope I do. I'd like it in blue."

At this, he frowned. "What are you talking about?"

"I don't know." I shrugged. "I thought we were talking about new trucks."

My unwillingness to join him in his childish game of supe shaming was irritating him now. "When are you going to fuck off and die?"

I tapped my chin in thought. "Probably about the same time you stop being a complete and utter asshole for no reason."

I tried to step around him, but he shoved his way back into my personal space. "I'm petitioning to have you stripped of your badge. You're living on borrowed time here."

I nudged Sawyer in the ribs with my elbow. "He used *petition* in a sentence like a big boy." Rolling my eyes, I added, "Look, why don't I let you get back to your date with your little boyfriend, Daye, and Sawyer and I will get back to solving cases."

At my insult, Daye's mouth fell open. He was as manly as a man got—volatile too. Actually, I had no idea how he'd made it onto the force in the first place. Daye curled his hand into a fist at his side and took a step forward.

My opal didn't react because it only reacted to supernatural threats, but Reaver did appear in my belt loop. Daye's too-closely-spaced eyes skimmed down my body to take in the huge sword I shouldn't be able to wield, then returned to my face.

"Next time, McKenzie," he threatened.

"Next time, what? You'll brush your teeth before coming to work? Because I know *everyone* would appreciate that."

He took another threatening step forward while Smith watched on smugly.

"I'd think very carefully about what you're about to do, Daye," Sawyer warned, his voice going all smoky and rough.

"Or what? You'll unleash your supernatural powers on me."

"Maybe he should." I pulled out my phone and pointed it in his direction, all ready for action. "I'd love to post a video of you violently and uncontrollably humping a fire hydrant."

Daye turned his scowl on me. Baring his teeth, he hissed, "You should've been kicked off the force for what you did."

"What *I* did? I didn't *do* anything."

"That's right," Smith sneered. "You didn't do a *goddam* thing."

Dammit, I walked right into that one. Even though I knew I shouldn't bite, I ground out, "I wasn't responsible for my partner's death, and I've had just about enough of people telling me that I was."

"You didn't do jack shit to save him."

"What the hell does that even mean, *jack shit?*" I took a sip of my coffee. "Argh, you guys are ruining my caffeine buzz." And with that, I turned and walked away.

"That was very restrained," Sawyer commented.

"I'm maturing."

We'd just walked into the PIG office when we both came to an abrupt stop. The office, which had only been occupied by Sawyer, Brax, and myself for the past week or so, was now overflowing with people.

Okay, maybe *overflowing* wasn't the right word. There were three new people. *Three.*

"What the ever-loving-fuck is going on?"

Sawyer stared at the newcomers and shook his head. "I have no idea."

"Think it's the new recruits like Wolfe was talking about?"

Before he could reply, Wolfe strolled into the room.

"Taylor, McKenzie, how's that werewolf case coming?"

"Good, sir. It's not a werewolf, though. It's the Amaroq."

Vaile's eyes flashed blue as Brax came to stand beside him. "Amaroq?" he asked.

"Inuit Legend. Turns into a wolf. Has *really* bad impulse control and enjoys spending his free time having murderous mantrums."

"How far away are you from catching the bastard?"

"Not too far," Sawyer said, walking over to his desk and perching on the edge. With nothing more to say to Wolfe, I followed Sawyer. After sliding off my jacket, I parked it on the edge of the pine beside my partner and waited.

My gaze shifted from the trio of strangers to Ben, who had walked through the door. His scowl was just as I remembered. Placing my coffee cup down, I raced up to him, throwing my arms around his neck. For some reason, I'd missed the snarling bastard.

He stiffened beneath me, then rumbled, "It's nice to see you, too, McKenzie, but get off me before I decide to revoke the *no eating the co-workers* rule I put in place just for you."

I squeezed him tightly one more time then stepped away, grinning. "You're back."

His gaze flickered to Brax then to Sawyer. "Yeah, I'm back."

"And now that he's back," Wolfe announced. "I'd like to introduce you all to the new recruits for PIG. This is Kayla." He nodded to a woman who looked no older than twenty-five. She had long, brown hair and the most stunning multi-hued eyes in shades of blue, green, and aqua. Kayla finger-waved to us and grinned.

"Pyro," he continued. Pyro had dark hair that danced with golden flames and gold eyes to match. He was also tall, but then again, most people were tall when compared to me.

And no, that wasn't bitterness in my voice.

"And Jacob." Jacob stared at me specifically, pushing some of his shoulder-length silver hair off his face. His skin looked as if it had been sprinkled in diamond dust, and on his back were a pair of onyx wings which he kept flaring like a peacock trying to attract a mate.

"They officially start work in the new year but have come in today to see how the office works, what the tempo is like, and for you to meet them." Turning to the trio, he said, "You'll eventually be assigned a partner, but for now, get to know each other. I'll check back in with you all in twenty."

Kayla gave Wolfe a mock salute. Pyro looked bored—and like he hadn't heard that at all—and Jacob was still looking at me, his eyes smoldering. Sawyer's hand was like a brand on my lower back as he glowered at the winged male.

Kayla sauntered over to us, her mini-skirt hiding just enough to be legal. She had on a pair of cowboy boots and a checkered shirt that had a few too many buttons undone in the front and a knot that flashed her bare midriff.

She scooped up my coffee cup and took a sip. "I prefer French roast," she said with a southern accent.

I snatched the cup from her hand. "You don't have boundaries, do you?"

"Nope."

I stared at her, trying to figure out what species of supe she was. "What are you?"

Flipping her hair from her shoulder, she smiled sweetly. "A harpy. And you?"

"Human," I gritted out.

Kayla's smile increased before her multi-hued eyes flickered to Sawyer. "What about you, hot-stuff?" She stepped closer to him, walking her hands up his chest. Sawyer's expression settled into cold indifference. "Ohhh, I know what you are," the harpy purred. "You're an incubus." She grabbed his crotch, and I seethed. Nobody touched what was mine. I watched the harpy's expression fall when Little Sawyer failed to rise to the occasion. "A defective incubus, though," she replied, removing her hand. It was a good thing too, because otherwise, I would've done it.

With Reaver.

"Too bad," Sawyer drawled, a muscle in his eye twitching.

She flounced off to what had been Hayliel's desk, perching on the edge. Jacob had already made himself at home there, but that arrogant smirk wasn't on his face anymore. He was staring down at the wood like he was being reunited with a loved one.

I switched my gaze to Pyro, who was still standing in the same spot, still had flames licking in his hair. He only looked to be about twenty-five or twenty-six too—the age all supes stopped aging—the lucky bastards.

"Why do I feel like we've just been made responsible for three puppies?" I asked Sawyer out of the corner of my mouth. "Three puppies who will insult, glower, and possibly burn anything and anyone around us."

"Because I think that's an apt description," Sawyer replied. "They're a little bit like you, actually."

I glared at him. "I was never this flippant." He arched a brow, and I huffed. "I mean, okay, yeah, maybe I was. But I wasn't obnoxious about it."

Again with an eyebrow lift.

Throwing my hands in the air, I huffed, "Argh, just forget about it." I stared at the new recruits. "Do you think they'll chew the furniture while we're out of the office?"

"What are we supposed to do now?" Kayla called from her perch on the desk. She was swinging her legs back and forth, back and forth, like a kid.

"I've got some paperwork you can file," I replied.

She leaped from the desk with a *harrumph* and sidled up to Brax's desk, pocketing his wallet when his back was turned. "I didn't join the cops to do paperwork. I want to get out there and gut some bad guys."

"We don't *gut* bad guys." Decapitate them, maybe, but definitely not gut.

Sawyer's phone rang.

"You could wash my car," Brax replied, smiling at her. "You can also put my wallet back."

Kayla flashed him a smile, reached into her back pocket and pulled out the leather billfold. She dropped it onto his desk with a flourish but swiped up a pack of gum as she hiked her hands back onto her hips.

"Cat? We have to go."

I turned to look at Sawyer. His expression was troubled. "What do we have?"

He stood, dumping his coffee cup in the trash. "Another missing person has been reported."

"Oh! I want to come!" Kayla said, jumping up and down. "I love dead bodies."

I glared at her. "That's wrong on so many levels. Besides, nobody said they were dead… just missing." I grabbed my jacket from the back of my chair, turning my back on her for just a moment. When I turned back to reach for my travel mug, it was gone.

I glanced around the room. Kayla was taking a sip, not meeting my eyes at all. "How in the hell did you get that?" I demanded.

"You didn't want it anymore."

"How do you figure?"

She shrugged. "You're leaving."

I looked over at Sawyer, who simply smiled at me with wry amusement. *He thought this was funny, did he?* "What's up with that?" I asked under my breath.

"Harpies can only eat and drink food that has been stolen or earned."

"She *stole* my coffee from me?"

Kayla flashed me a smile. "Yeah, and if you don't want anything else stolen by me, you'd best not leave your shit laying around."

"It was hardly—"

"Come on, pussy cat," Sawyer murmured into my ear. "Being on a harpy's bad side isn't how you want to start your Monday."

"You're right. I'd rather start it with a coffee."

"Who is it this time?" I asked into the comms system, clinging to Sawyer's body as we rounded a tight bend. We were driving up the mountain road, the switchbacks causing the coffee in my stomach to roil.

"A construction worker didn't report in for work this morning."

"So, they filed a missing person report?"

"Yes. But given the location and the history of this place, I think it's safe to assume it's not somebody we're going to find alive."

It bothered me to no end that the Amaroq was getting away with this, but we had no idea where the guy hid when he wasn't viciously killing people in a petulant rage because he was woken up early from a nap.

When we finally reached the plateau, Sawyer slowed his bike and pulled into a vacant spot in the parking lot. Construction trucks surrounded us, the sides of their bodies splashed with mud and crusted salt.

We found Gregory behind the reception desk, dressed in casual clothes and without his usual groomed-to-within-an-inch-of-his-life perfection. There was stubble across his cheeks and jaw, and large black circles under his eyes.

"Thank you for coming so quickly."

"No problem. When was the man last seen?"

"After dinner last night. Many of the workers are staying here while construction is taking place, and since the lodge is empty now anyway, it seemed like the easiest solution."

"Around what time was dinner?"

"Six-thirty. Mr. Simons was last seen between seven-thirty and eight."

"Where?" I asked, wincing at the sound of circular saws and air nail guns in the background.

Gregory waited until the sawing stopped. "Apparently, he stepped outside to have a cigarette. He was supposed to be playing cards with some of his friends but never showed up to their room."

"Could he have gone somewhere else? Returned home, maybe?"

Gregory shook his head. "All these workers are from another state. The owner of the lodge is friends with the primary contractor, and a special deal was struck. His friend got to use his men rather than local labor, and Mr. Scali agreed to accommodate all the workers."

"Speaking of the owner," I said. "He's not going to stop construction, is he?"

"No. I relayed your concerns to him, but he said something about not listening to a cop about business matters."

It was a dead-end trying to get the owner to shut things down, which meant it was up to Sawyer and me to catch the Amaroq before he could kill any more people.

"We'll take a look around, Greg. Keep the body bag ready."

He startled. "Body bag?"

"What's the plan of attack?" I asked as Sawyer made his way to the door.

"*Officer*, what body bag?" Gregory called after us.

Sawyer continued on as if he hadn't heard him, exiting the lobby and walking a few paces away. Staring at the forest, he said, "We need to find Mr. Simon's body."

"You're assuming we're going to find a body rather than find him alive."

"You're stalling."

"Of course, I'm stalling." I gestured to the tree line. "I already know what I'm going to find in there. I know I *have to* go in there, but I need a little time to, you know, gain the courage. I didn't put on my unicorn panties this morning." Clearly an oversight on my end.

"Detective Taylor?"

We both turned to see Gregory in the doorway.

"What's up, Greg?" I asked.

"The wife of the missing man is on the phone. She demanded to speak with the detective on the case. I tried to get her to calm down, but she's hysterical and—"

"It's fine. I'll take the call." Sawyer looked at me.

I heaved a sigh. "Run along then. I'll wait for you and sulk for a bit longer."

With a determined nod, Sawyer strode back inside, leaving me alone in the cold morning air. I scanned the trees in front of me, trying to figure out whether going in there would end terribly for me.

My opal suddenly flared brightly, my spine straightening when I heard the chatter of wood sprites.

Dammit, we were already too late.

Unclipping my Glock, I held the firearm down by my side and moved forward. My instincts immediately flared to life, warning me that this was a bad, bad idea. As if I needed another reminder of just *how* badly this could end, my opal started to pulse, the light getting brighter and brighter the deeper I ventured into the forest.

I began to jog, dodging low-lying branches and hurdling over logs felled by storms or heavy snowfall. The snow that had made it down to the ground created some patches of ground slick, and a couple of times, I almost went over. It was when I saw Sage and her merry band of flying sharks that I really began to panic. If the wood sprites were here, it could only mean that the Amaroq had rung the dinner bell.

The forest god has provided again! one of Sage's harem declared joyfully.

He is merciful. He is kind to us, said another.

Jesus, these creatures had to get out more.

Actually, on second thought, maybe not...

I skidded to a stop when I saw a figure crouched down in the snow, his arms upraised like he was trying to fend off an invisible attack. My eyes darted around the clearing, looking for any signs of the Amaroq. When I was confident it was clear, I stepped past the tree I was hiding—err, *standing*—behind and approached the guy.

"Sir? Sir? Hey, are you all right?" I asked, holstering my Glock and touching him on the shoulder. I immediately withdrew my hand. His skin was ice-cold, pale, and hard to the touch. It was almost like he was frozen, but there weren't any ice crystals on his skin. With my heart trying to climb out of my throat, I edged around him to see his face.

The first thing that struck me was he was only young—maybe in his mid to late twenties. The second thing was his expression. His eyes were wide open, his mouth set in a gaping scream. Inside his mouth, his tongue had been bitten in two, the blood also frozen solid. Even though it disgusted me, I grabbed a stick from the ground and probed a little farther. He wasn't missing a tooth like the others, so what were we dealing with?

The same killer or a copycat?

If it was the same killer, the MO had changed once more. This guy hadn't been used as a chew toy.

She's touching our breakfast!

I looked down to find the wood sprites hovering near the man's stomach. They'd torn through his clothing then burrowed into his abdominal cavity, feasting on his flesh as I stood there and gawked.

"You guys need to work on your table manners," I muttered.

One of the males flashed a pair of sharp teeth at me before diving back inside the body cavity.

Ick. *Ick*. ICK.

"Sage, what's going on?"

Sage popped out of the hole they'd made, her entire body covered in blood and gore. Somehow blood trickled from the edge of the wound, the dark liquid *tap, tap, tapping* to the snowy ground between us. Apparently, he wasn't frozen *solid*.

Oh, it's you again, she snarked.

"Don't give me that attitude. What happened?"

Petrified.

Petrified? Clearly, the guy was terrified when he died. You couldn't pass that expression off as anything else. "Thank you for stating the obvious." I ran a hand through my hair. "When did you find him?"

Last night. We heard a commotion. When there's a commotion in the forest, we come. It means food will be waiting for us.

"Has this happened before? Before today? In the past?"

Sage got a dreamy look on her face. *Oh, yes. There was a time when the forest god provided for us every day, but then he left, and we were left to feed on animals.* She ran her twig-like finger down the torso of the construction worker. *Human flesh is so much sweeter.*

"I should get you together with Ben. You two would get on like a house on fire." I let out a sigh. "Do you know where the *forest god* goes when he's not home delivering for you and your posse?"

Sage shook her tiny head. A tiny flower dropped off from her hair and floated slowly to the ground. *We do not know.* She folded her arms and began tapping her foot. *Are we finished talking now?*

I waved her away. "Yeah. Go finish the all-you-can-eat." There was no point in trying to stop it from happening now. "You only have until my partner gets here."

She pouted at me. *I miss the times when we could pick the carcass completely clean without interruption.*

"Wait. What?"

But Sage ignored me, diving back into the cavity like there was wood sprite crack in there.

Maybe there was.

Pulling out my phone, I dialed Sawyer and wandered to the edge of the clearing. "Found the guy."

"Where are you? Outside the lodge?"

I looked at the tall trees surrounding me. "Nah, a little farther afield than that."

"You said you'd wait for me."

"I heard the wood sprites and came to investigate."

He growled, the sound sending a shower of sparks through me. Before he could chew me out, though, I said, "I know. Dangerous. Stupid move, McKenzie."

He bit out, "I'm still on the phone with the widow. "Just stay where you are. I'll find you."

"Roger that." I hung up, then frowned at the mist that was slowly seeping in between the trees and crawling along the ground.

Mist.

Mist was bad...

A dark shadow fell over me, and I stiffened.

My opal flared hot.

Moving slowly, I reached for my Glock even though every single one of my instincts was firing. Holding the weapon down at my side, I turned to face the Amaroq...

... only it *wasn't* the Amaroq.

It was something much bigger...

16

"Spider. Spider," I chanted in a hoarse whisper. How I was able to speak was beyond me. All the moisture felt like it had been siphoned out of my mouth. "*Huge* spider. *Huge!*" I whispered to myself.

Adrenaline shot through my system, careening out of control and making my heart race. I gasped, trying to draw in a breath, but the feeling of being smothered was too real—pressing against my chest. The overgrown spider in front of me took up all the available space in the clearing, clear liquid beading from the tips of its six-foot fangs.

Dizzy—trembling—I forced myself to ease back a step to put some distance between us and as I did, I saw that there was a thick swath of material stretched over its eyes.

It was... *blindfolded?*

Who in the hell had put a blindfold on a spider? That was like trying to tie a bow around the leg of a fly—seemingly impossible—but they were obviously a determined son of a bitch.

I did a quick scan of the rest of its body. Between its thorax and abdomen, there was a thin, gold band. *A slave band?* Who would want a huge spider as their slave? I mean, great for clearing a room, re-creating the movie *Arachnophobia*, or at Halloween, but at any other time?

Movement from the corner of my eye caught my notice, and I slapped a hand over my mouth to silence my whimpering. Thousands upon thousands of spiders scrambled along the ground and in the trees, moving in my direction.

As I eased back another step, I trod on a twig, flinching when the sharp crack resembled a gunshot in the mid-morning air. The spider's attention changed, the small appendages at the front of its body tapping the ground where I had been, then slowly moving in my direction. I lifted my Glock, took aim then let out a breath before firing at its palpitating legs.

The spider screamed. Not letting go of my gun, I awkwardly threw my hands over my ears, watching the giant arachnid rear backward. I ran for the cover of the trees, hiding behind one then peering out.

Sawyer would've heard that shot. He would come.

Shucking my jacket, I threw it into the clearing in the hopes that the spider wouldn't know the difference. It would retain the warmth of my body for a few minutes, and it would smell like me. Maybe it would mistake my jacket for me. Maybe...

... not.

The spider, seemingly recovered from the GSW, stalked forward, ignoring the bundle of red leather. It scampered all over the clearing, its palps working the snowy ground. It felt its way along the trees, moving closer. For half a second, I thought it wouldn't find me. For half a second, I thought I could beat the humungous blind spider. I mean, it seemed like a no-brainer, but it moved like it *could* see, like all its other senses were working to make up for the deficit. It was coming toward me now, so I bolted farther into the trees, hoping the extra obstacles would slow it down. No such luck. If anything, the arachnid seemed to be getting faster.

Well, I wasn't going down like this.

Refocusing on what was in front of me, I pumped my arms and ran a little faster, vaulting over logs and shrubs. I risked one more look behind me, knowing the spider would be there…

It wasn't.

And that's how I ran straight into a huge web suspended between two widely spaced trees. The instant I hit the silk, I was caught. No wiggling to get out. No way to reach for Reaver who had *finally* appeared and was propped in the fork of a tree just out of reach.

Typical.

The web bounced violently, and I strained my neck to see how far away from certain death I was.

Oh, good news!

Only about five more seconds.

The spider crept slowly down the web, going for maximum terror. I strained against the steel-like strength of the spider silk, trying to wrench myself free. My opal flared, putting on another heat and light show, and I had to wonder what would happen now. Would it repel an attack like it had with Kseniya or would it do something equally unexpected?

The spider reached out one leg and glided it down my arm…

Free me.

I stopped struggling when I heard the words pushed into my head.

Again, the spider stroked my arm, then my cheek. Gently. Like it didn't want to hurt me.

Free me.

The tone was beseeching—sad.

Tilting my head up, I stared at the spider. Was it *talking* to me?

Free me… please.

Frowning, I croaked, "I—"

Fire.

There was fire in my veins. Holding back a scream, I looked down to see the spider had run its fang—and the poison dripping from it— against my bicep. My skin was instantly red raw, bubbling and hissing as the poison worked its way through my bloodstream.

My head started to swim, and all I could think was that this was it. This really was my time. But as soon as my thoughts appeared, they disappeared in a rush of sharp pain and even sharper agony.

"Why…" Why was my head so foggy? And was my chest rising and falling jaggedly? I tried again to speak. "Why… w-w-whyyy…" I blinked, my vision suddenly joining up with Hazy and Spotty. I was vaguely aware of my opal flaring so brightly it was like standing beside the noon-day sun, but then…

… there was only darkness.

17

I was floating in a sea of darkness. It was cold here. So cold. I was shivering—at least I thought I was. It was hard to know what was what. If I was having thoughts, I couldn't be dead, but why was it so dark?

And where was Sawyer?

"I'm right here, pussy cat," a voice that sounded a lot like Sawyer's said, except panic threaded through the tone. "I'm going to help you, okay, but I need you to swallow what I give you."

Swallow? "Now isn't the time for a blow job," I mumbled.

"The spider's venom…" He took a deep breath. "It's working through you. I don't know how you're still alive right now."

"Spider…" I breathed out the word. That's right. I was stuck in its web, and it had *spoken* to me. "Spider," I mumbled, my lips starting to feel numb. "Big. Huge. The hugest."

"That's not a word, pussy cat," he gently chastised.

"Hey, I'm the one dying here. I can make up words."

"You. Are. *Not*. Dying. Do you hear me?"

I let out a sigh and rolled my face in the direction of his voice. "How can you stop me, huh? It feels like I'm dying. It's black, and I'm all floaty."

"Pussy cat, I *need* you to swallow, okay? It will make you better."

"Just make sure it's coffee and add loads of sugar. I want coffee to be the last thing I drink."

Sawyer moved away from me. I didn't know how I knew—the air just felt different, colder somehow. I tried to lift my arms and legs, but they were like lead. I couldn't even open my eyes, but the darkness was good. I could deal with darkness.

There was a hiss, then, "Open your mouth for me, pussy cat," Sawyer said in a strained voice.

I opened my mouth and waited for the sweet, smoky taste of coffee to hit my tongue, but that was not what I got. Instead, I tasted something metallic. It was like swallowing old pennies. When I tried to spit it out, Sawyer held my mouth closed and pinched my nose. As weak as I was, I tried to push him off me. I struggled weakly in his arms, my lungs starting to burn as whatever he'd put in my mouth slowly dripped into the back of my throat.

Blood.

It was blood, I realized with horror.

My lungs screamed at me now, and I had no choice but to swallow, to get the air that I needed. I gasped, dragging in the oxygen I'd been deprived.

"I'm so sorry, pussy cat," Sawyer said in a soft voice. His lips pressed against my temple and mumbled, "So sorry. So sorry. So sorr—"

My spine bowed without warning as pain ricocheted through my entire body. I opened my mouth to ask him what was happening, but all that came out was a scream. Pain like I'd never felt before shot through my body like quicksilver. My arms and legs flopped around, their movements completely out of my control. I managed to pry my eyes open. Sawyer was still holding me, the muscles in his neck taut as he tried to keep me still.

"W-W-What did you do?" I managed to slur out, the numbness was not only in my lips anymore but on my tongue too.

He gazed down at me with stormy gray eyes. "I don't know… There was just this *instinct*."

Moaning, I flailed weakly in his hold, feeling as if my entire body had been doused in gasoline and lit on fire. I drank his blood. What was it going to do to me? And WTF was that instinct line about? Argh, supernaturals!

I lost track of time but thrashing uncontrollably would do that to you. All I knew was there was pain, and then there was *this* pain, which was the worst I'd ever felt. Every one of my muscles was taut, straining painfully over my bones. Bones which felt like the marrow had been sucked out and replaced by acid. By tomorrow—if I ever *lived* to tomorrow—I'd wish I was dead.

Sawyer smoothed the hair out of my eyes, cooing to me gently. I tried to focus on his face. Was this what women in labor felt like when they stared at their husband or partner while working through a contraction? It was like intense—love coupled with a burning hatred that they had put you in this position to start with.

Love? Why was I even contemplating that right now? What did I love? That jacket. I hope Sawyer picked it up for me.

"My jacket…" I started, my words dropping away as unconsciousness claimed me.

When I woke up again, the pain was—thankfully—gone. I blinked up to find Sawyer still cradling me in his arms.

"Pussy cat?" he asked in a croak.

"Yeah?"

Relief made his gray eyes shine. It was so palpable, in fact, that I could've sworn I felt my chest warm up with the emotion. "Oh, thank fuck you're alive."

I tried to shift into a sitting position because I hated having conversations like this while I was flat on my back. He helped me up, keeping his arm locked around me.

We were in the lobby of the lodge. "Why wouldn't I be alive?"

He glanced up, wincing when a jackhammer started *rat-a-tat-a-tatting* in the construction area. Ignoring my question, he said, "I carried you here."

"And why wouldn't I be alive?" I pressed more aggressively.

He shook his head, his expression regretful. "I didn't know what would happen. I reacted on impulse, which was stupid because I had no idea how fast the venom would work through your body. Feeding you my blood could've killed you even faster.

I brushed a hand over my arm where the spider had bitten. There was a faint line about a foot long running down my bicep, but other than that, nobody would be able to tell what had happened.

I skated my hand over my body, checking for other injuries, and when it landed on my chest, I winced. Sawyer peeled my hand away.

"There's quite a bad burn there. Your opal was glowing hot and bright the whole time."

"Why didn't it work like it did with Kseniya?" I wondered out loud. When the witch had attacked me, it had deflected the blows. This was a life-or-death situation too. "I'm getting tired of sentient objects," I groused.

"She was using magic on you. This spider, however unnaturally big, is still a natural thing, unlike Kseniya's magic."

I looked at Sawyer's wrist and forearm. Blood was smeared all over. I pointed. "You've got red on you."

He tucked his arm away out of sight.

"Why did you feed me your blood?"

For a long time, he didn't reply—he only stared at me.

"Come on, Sawyer, the suspense is killing me."

He winced at my choice of words. "I was trying to save you. The venom was... I could feel the spark of your life draining away, and I couldn't let that happen. So I fed you my blood. I..." He hesitated. "I didn't know the pain you would experience would be so intense."

I frowned. "Was the pain from the venom burning out of my system or from your blood?"

"No." He brushed some hair behind my ear. "The pain was a new connection forming... with me."

I blinked. "Run that by me again?"

He sighed, suddenly looking tired and relieved at the same time. "Yesterday morning—"

"Before the Adventures in Spideyland," I added helpfully.

He gave me a tight nod. "I spoke with the elf who has been looking into human consorts for me. He found out that there was a way for an incubus and a human to have the same lifespan… by forming a life bond."

"A life bond," I repeated. Rubbing at my chest like it was suddenly tight.

"Yes. For supernatural consorts, this isn't a necessity, but since you're human…" He shrugged, looking almost apologetic.

I sucked in a breath and let it go. "How was this life bond formed?"

"I bit you."

I shivered as I remembered the feeling of his teeth in me. "Yes." My word was breathy and filled with longing.

Did I enjoy being bitten by him? Clearly, the answer was yes.

"I drank from you."

"Yes."

"And today, I fed you some of my blood."

I nodded to show I was picking up what he was putting down. "And by feeding me your blood, you completed the life bond?"

He studied me intently, his question burning in his eyes. "How… how do you feel about that? I know I should've told you what I'd learned from the elf, but…"

I let the knowledge settle over me.

How did I feel? Right now, I was grateful that he'd saved my life, but

I had to know more.

"What does this bond entail?"

He let out a breath and stroked my thigh. "It means that your lifeforce is tied to mine. If I die, you die. If you die, I die. There can't be one without the other."

I swallowed roughly. "What else?"

"As far as what else might happen to us, I don't know. The elf didn't elaborate much more than he knew it was possible. The consequences of this bond will be unknown until they appear."

"That sounds… random and potentially dangerous. A lot like my life."

"It's not without its risks, pussy cat, but you're worth it." He squeezed my hand. "You're my other half, and I'd die if I didn't have you in my life."

"Quite literally now," I deadpanned. Our lives were entwined forever. It was the kind of commitment most women would kill to have in their lives. Granted my bond was with a supe, but Sawyer was the man for me. He just got me. Plus, he was amazing in bed.

Bonus.

"So, what do you think?" he asked in a soft voice. "I didn't ask you if you wanted this, but I couldn't sit there and watch you die."

"Am I jazzed that I drank your blood? No. *Gack.* But am I okay with the fact that I'm still alive so I can keep you on your toes? You betcha."

Now all I had to do was convince myself of this.

"Thank you, pussy cat," he murmured. "Thank you."

Man, I had to lighten the serious mood. "Think I'll grow any taller now that we're bound together?"

He gave me a wry grin. "No."

"Super strength?"

"Probably not."

"The ability to collect more unicorn paraphernalia?"

"I don't think you need a life bond to do that. You do that all on your own."

I winked. "I am pretty awesome, right?"

18

We returned to our apartment, Sawyer not letting me out of his sight for a moment.

"You should rest," he told me, trying to lead me into his bedroom.

I raised an eyebrow at him. "If I need to rest, I should do it in my own bed, right? Surrounded by my own things."

He shook his head, determination shining in his gray eyes. "No. I want you with me all the time now." At my raised brow, he added, "To make sure you're safe."

"I believe that's called paranoia." *Was this a side effect of the bond?* "Why wouldn't I be safe in my own room? Afraid the unicorn statues will come to life because, believe me, I'd probably pee my pants in excitement if they did."

The muscle in his jaw feathered with his annoyance, and I swore I felt that annoyance singing through my own veins.

"Besides, what about Lee?" I asked. "And the CSI. They still have to work the scene."

"I'll call the ME and CSI, and send Brax to meet them there while you rest."

"I'm actually feeling pretty good," I replied. "*We* could meet them there."

My stubborn, infuriating, sexy-as-fuck incubus stared at me for a full minute, his mouth thinning into a mulish line. "You could've *died* an hour ago."

"But I didn't. I need to celebrate that."

"By walking *back into* the danger zone?"

Doing my best *Austin Powers* impression, I replied, "Danger is my middle name."

He snorted. "No, it's not. It's Ellen."

"I told you not to share that around," I hissed. "I still have to have some mystery about me."

He made a production of looking around our apartment. "There's nobody else here," he pointed out. "And you could celebrate it by resting in my bed while *I* organize for the body to be taken care of."

I snorted, pushing past him into my room. I was in the walk-in closet pulling a thick winter coat off a hanger when he stalked in behind me. Peering at him over my shoulder, I said, "I'm going back. You can either come with me or stay behind, but you know how much trouble I get into when I'm unsupervised."

Sawyer folded his arms and rested his shoulder against the jamb, heaving a sigh. "Why do you have to make everything so difficult?"

I blinked at him. *Did I just win the round?* Tentatively, I asked, "Does this mean—"

"Yes, but only on one condition."

Oh. I deflated. "What?"

"You rest first. Then eat. *Then* we go."

I didn't point out that he'd stated two conditions. I took my wins when I could.

"Fine."

THREE HOURS OF SLEEP, TWO SANDWICHES, AND ONE INFURIATINGLY fussy incubus later, we were back on Sawyer's bike and heading up to the lodge. We were both dressed in thick jackets, waterproof pants, and fur-lined boots, ready for traipsing through the forest.

"Are you sure you're ready for this?" Sawyer asked through the comms.

I shrugged, hugging myself closer to the safety of his body. "Sure. I haven't been in any life-threatening situations since... this morning. I'm about due for one."

He huffed. "You really do have a morbid sense of humor."

"You knew this going in."

By the time we arrived back on the mountain, a sense of foreboding was sitting heavily in my stomach, making those two sandwiches Sawyer had forced me to eat churn in my gut.

"Are you sure you're ready?" Sawyer asked for the umpteenth time.

I sucked in a breath and let it go. I couldn't get angry at him. He was merely concerned for my health, which meant he was concerned for *his* health. "Sure. Why not?"

"Because if you want to go back to the apartment and rest, you can. I can handle this one on my own."

I shrugged and began walking around the side of the lodge, Sawyer following behind me. I surveyed the forest. We had to find the Amaroq, but where in the hell did we start looking?

"Sawyer, I know you're afraid of me getting hurt, but if we're in this together, you need to let me do my job."

"I'm not trying to stop—"

"*Yes*, you are. I'm not some fragile doll who will break at the slightest bump. I have a bad-ass angelic sword and an opal that repels magic."

"And you're *human*."

I snorted. "Since when has that ever stopped me?"

He shook his head, then pressed a kiss to my lips. A warm, languid heat filled me at his touch. "Just… I want you to stay safe, okay?"

"Don't I always?"

He heaved a sigh. "No. You don't. So please try to keep out of trouble."

I gave him a salute. "I promise I won't do anything reckless."

"And at the first sign of danger, I want you to run."

"Believe me, if spiders are involved, I'll be hauling ass out of there."

We started down the same walking track that led to where my truck had been unceremoniously dumped, the silence of the forest pressing against us. It was like even the birds weren't brave enough to sing. The deeper we ventured, the thicker the trees grew. As soon as the mist rolled in, I knew we were getting closer.

"Stay in front of me," Sawyer commanded in a harsh bark. "I'll watch our backs. And keep Reaver up."

I would've blown it off, but his concern sprung from fear, and I got it. There was a lot more at stake here than just my life now. "Roger that."

Raising the sword, it phosphoresced steadily, joining the glow from my opal. Like before, the mist stayed away from me. Sawyer, on the other hand, wasn't so lucky. He cursed every few moments as he pulled the tendrils away from his exposed skin.

Moving forward, I led the way deeper into the forest until an itch began to form between my shoulder blades.

"Can you feel that, Sawyer?"

"Yes. We're being hunted."

"Fantastic. I'll tick that off my *Twenty Ways to Die* bingo sheet."

To distract myself from the feeling of impending doom, I kept my gaze moving, straining my ears to see if I could hear the dolphin-like chatter of the wood sprites.

The forest was still silent, though.

Eerily quiet.

"The Amaroq isn't being a very good host," I whispered, raising my sword a little higher when I heard a noise. After I was sure it wasn't anything more than my imagination, I muttered to myself, "Letting us wander around out here on our own."

"I think he's just herding us to where he wants us."

"Which is where? The corner of Scared Mindless Avenue and Ticked Off Street? Because I'm sooo already there." I shivered. "All we need to do is find out wherever the hell this Amaroq stays when he's not tenderizing campers and arrest his ass."

"Easier said than done," he gritted out.

"If the wood sprites were here, I could ask them."

"If the wood sprites were here..." Sawyer started, "... we'd be dealing with another body."

Dammit, he was right.

I scanned the forest once more. The mist had grown thicker, so thick in fact that I could hardly see six feet in front of me—even with the glow of Reaver.

That was when I saw it.

A little ball of electric blue light hovering just above the ground.

"Wisp," Sawyer said softly into my ear, the heat of his body warming my back.

"Murderous Ball of Light is a better name for it," I bitched while stepping a little closer to it. The wisp shifted back the same distance. "Please don't tell me it wants us to follow it."

"It wants us to follow it."

I gave him the stink-eye. "I told you not to tell me that."

He shrugged, his amusement hovering in the air between us. "Doesn't change the fact that it does." He pointed at the wisp. "Keep Reaver in front of you. I'll cover your back."

Reaver hummed in anticipation—another sign that things were about to go south. The sword got excited at the prospect of bloodshed, and who was I to deny it those little pleasures?

We followed the will-o'-the-wisp for at least half a mile, traversing ground that seemed to morph from flat land and trees to inclines and boulders. Soon, we were scrambling over the oversized rocks, the grip on the bottom of my shoes not doing much to keep traction. Visibility didn't improve either, our line of vision reducing to just a couple of feet.

When another wisp joined the first, then another, and another, I turned to Sawyer. "Extra wisps aren't good, are they? I mean, less is more?"

"Shh." Sawyer pointed. "Look."

I *did* look and wished I hadn't. The wisps were all moving toward something black—a murky void hidden in the thick mist.

I realized it was the mouth of a cave, and I swallowed. Hard. "You think we need to go in there?"

"That's where the wisps are leading us."

"You said wisps lead travelers to their doom," I hissed back, my pulse rate starting to spike.

"They do."

"Not making me feel any better here, Sawyer."

"You'll be fine, pussy cat. Just keep going."

Grumbling to myself, I clambered over huge stones and weaved between the sparse trees growing among them. When I stepped over a fallen log, I tripped on the other side—my foot getting caught in between some rocks. Reaching around, I tried to free the toe of my boot and caught a flash of bleached white. Frowning, I brushed away the dirt and pebbles.

"It's a bone," I told him. "Old. Look."

He inched a little closer to investigate then checked around, eyes narrowing on the mountain face in front of us.

I scanned the rocks. Holy shit. "There are *hundreds* of them. Look."

I pushed the dirt from another patch of bleached bone and recoiled. It was a skull. "Definitely human," I told him, pointing.

"I think we may have found the bodies of all those construction workers from thirty-five years ago." Standing, he offered me his hand and pulled me back onto my feet. "Are you okay?"

I brushed some snow off the seat of my pants. "Well, if you include the fact that we're following balls of light to our certain doom, then yeah, I'm good."

One of the will-o'-the-wisps floated closer, zipping around us both before joining the other glowing balls of electric blue a few feet away.

"I've never seen a wisp act like this," Sawyer said, staring at the now half a dozen light balls hovering above the ground.

"Oh, great, so they're acting weird and multiplying? Like in the movie *Gremlins*? That's just what I need."

"Come on," he urged, placing his hand at the small of my back. We continued to follow the wisps, climbing higher and higher until we were at least fifty feet off the ground.

"If we're being led to our deaths, I'm going to be very unhappy," I grouched, finding another foothold before lifting myself onto a small ledge where I could rest.

"Just keep going," Sawyer gritted out.

I peered up over the next rock shelf and sighed in relief. The wisps had stopped moving, but they were hovering in front of the cave's entrance. Pulling myself up and over the edge, I waited for Sawyer, helping him up.

I looked at the dark maw of the cave opening and shivered. An arctic wind blew out from it, the coppery scent of blood on the air.

The wisps extinguished their lights in front of our faces, leaving us alone.

"I'm not going in there," I said out loud. "Nope, no way in—" A shrill, terrified scream cut through my words. "Hell," I finished.

Sawyer pulled out his Glock. "That sounded human."

"How can you tell?"

"*Come on.*"

"Come on *where?*" I gestured to the dark-and-scary cave opening. "I'm not going in there. Nothing good comes from darkness and terrified screams."

Sawyer worked his jaw for a moment before saying, "You're right. You stay here, and I'll go in." He took two steps before I grabbed his arm and pulled him to a stop.

"Whoa, whoa, whoa. You think *I'm* going to stay out here while you go in there?"

"It'll be safer."

"Safer? Safer f—" My phone rang, and I yanked it out of my pocket. "*What?*"

"She's gone!" a woman screamed into the receiver. "Rachel's gone!"

"Mrs. Hayes?" I asked, turning to look at Sawyer.

"She was taken from her hospital room last night. I don't know where she is. She's just gone."

Another scream echoed from the cave in front of us, and I knew.

"Mrs. Hayes, I'll call you back."

19

My opal pulsed to the same rhythm of my heart, the increasing pace making my mouth dry. Why was Rachel inside a cave in the middle of the forest when she should be in the hospital right now?

"How?" was all I could ask Sawyer.

He shook his head. "She was either taken from the room, or she left on her own."

"Her leg was still in traction. How in the hell was a thirteen-year-old girl supposed to get out of her hospital bed and come here?"

The muscle in his jaw feathered as he ground out, "I don't know."

Another horrified scream punctured the air. It didn't matter *how* she got there, just that she was. "Come on."

I stepped into the cave and whispered to Reaver, "Light this bitch up."

The sword began to glow, the cool blue light illuminating the cave and creating shadows on the walls that seemed to move even though I was standing still. Oh, wait, the walls *were* moving…

… with about a bazillion spiders.

I quickly moved away from them. My fear response threatened to take over, but I took in a deep breath and let it out.

Sawyer stepped beside me, his Glock out at the ready. "Are you okay?"

"I will be as long as none of them touch me."

The wind that barreled through the cave was colder than what was outside, the scent of blood and old, dead things growing thicker by the second.

I shuffled my feet along the cold, stone floor, loose pebbles shifting with every step. They rolled this way and that, some falling and bouncing—their journey amplified by the cave's curved roof. When we came to a clear bend in the cave system, I hesitated.

Running head-long into danger *did* seem to be my jam, but damn, sometimes it took me some time to get the guts up to do it.

It was another one of those screams that got me moving again. The girl sounded terrified. Pushing forward, I cringed away from the wall when I brushed past something sticky. Holding Reaver up, I saw that the whole thing was covered in spider webs.

Well, at least the tiny spiders were gone.

Hooray.

My breath hovering in front of my face as I whispered, "We're in the spider's nest."

Another scream.

And Sawyer and I both broke into a run—spider webs be damned.

Around another corner, we both stopped abruptly. Rachel was on the ground in the middle of a cavern, her broken leg out in front of her. Blood dripped from a gash above her eye, but it was the look of abject fear on her face that did it for me. She was staring at something I couldn't see yet, but as soon as her gaze found mine, she broke down into a fresh wave of sobs.

"Cat," she moaned.

"I'm here, Rachel," I told her, running in her direction. I dropped Reaver when I reached her, smoothing my hands over her hair and inspecting the wound. "What the hell happened?"

"A man came into my room last night and took me from the hospital. I tried to fight him off, but it was like nobody else could see or hear him. He left me here with… with… *her.*"

"Who?"

Anansssi.

My opal flared as the word echoed in my head. I spun around, searching past the darkness that still blanketed some corners of the cave. Scooping up Reaver, I stood and faced the darkest shadow.

"Come out," I demanded, biting my bottom lip to stop it quivering. Without turning around, I added, "Sawyer, get Rachel out of here."

"No. Cat—"

"Sawyer!" I begged. If Rachel was injured any more, I could never forgive myself. "Just get her out of here. *Please.*"

"You promised you wouldn't put yourself in danger," he hissed. "It's not just your life at stake here."

I turned to glare at him. As if I needed the freaking reminder. "I know, and we can discuss this later." I held his eyes, begging him silently. "Just get her out of here. I can stall until you get back."

With a soft growl I knew well, he scooped up Rachel and removed her from the cave.

When I was confident he was gone, I let out a breath and squinted into the gloom. "Come out," I called. Reaver's glow only seemed to penetrate so far into the cave. There was a definite block there. "Come out, Anansi."

The shadows shifted, moving like liquid smoke. Eight long legs, a swollen abdomen, two gleaming fangs and... a blindfold over the eyes.

You, she said into my head, her front legs palpitating the ground.

"Me. Why did you have the girl?"

Keeping her safe from the wolf.

"From the Amaroq?"

Yes. He wishes to keep her for his own.

I licked my lips. "And what about you?" I eased a few steps to the right, and her whole body moved with me. "Why are you here and blindfolded?"

I am his prisoner.

That last word echoed around us as she reared up, revealing the five-inch-thick gold band wrapped around her thorax.

"He keeps you here? The Amaroq?"

To do his bidding, yes. I am trapped just as much as that girl was.

"Where is he now?"

Because that bad wolf was going to get a spanking.

He'll return soon.

"And what'll happen when he does?"

He's going to bite the child—create another of his kind—in order to build an army against the humans.

Jesus. The Amaroq was more ambitious than I gave him credit for. "*Where* is he?"

"I'm right here," the Amaroq said in a smug voice. "Catherine. Ellen. McKenzie."

I spun around, shielding my eyes as the entire cave was suddenly illuminated by thousands upon thousands of fireflies covering the cave's ceiling. The Amaroq looked just the same as before, only there was a three-gouge scratch down his cheek. I grinned knowing Rachel had to have been the one to give it to him.

"Couldn't handle a little girl, I see. I thought you would've healed that already."

He touched the wound gently. "The girl has spirit. It means she'll survive my bite."

"Why did you abduct her?"

He began to circle around me, my opal pulsing in warning. "She was returning to me when the dryad found her." He bared his teeth in a fierce scowl. "Then you came and took her away again. I had to wait to collect her once more."

I swung Reaver around to keep it between us. "Why would she return to you?"

"She saw what I did to her brother. She wanted her revenge on me, but I knew I was going to keep her. She didn't once look away when I slashed his throat or stomach. Not once did she scream. She is the perfect choice to receive my bite."

"She was *in shock*, you monster."

"No, she wasn't. She was *fascinated*. I spoke into her mind then, asking if she would come and find me. She said she would but then *you* found her after she'd hurt herself. You took her away from me."

"Wait, I'm confused. You were doing all this for a thirteen-year-old girl?" If he did, that was messed up.

He growled at me, the noise sounding unnatural coming from a human throat. "No, I was doing this so I could stop the humans from invading any more of my home. There's so much noise now—humans on snowmobiles, tearing up the forest, yelling, camping, parties." He flung his hand out in the direction of the lodge, spittle flying from his lips. "Thirty-five years ago, I had to take man after man to stop that noise. And now it's started again."

"So how was Rachel going to help you with your little *human* sprawl problem, huh? Raise money by selling Girl Scout cookies? No, it was with a rinky-dink lemonade stand out the front of her house, right?" I laughed in his face. "You want to know what I think? I think Rachel was the only one to witness you making a kill, and you needed to get rid of her."

He shook his head, and I noticed the beads he'd woven into his hair. Wait. *Not* beads, but teeth. Most were yellow with age, but there were at least two white ones.

He *was* collecting trophies.

Well, bully for him.

"There's just one thing I don't know."

"What's that?" he sneered.

"You had your chance to kill me after the spider dropped me into the middle of the forest. Why didn't you?"

He seethed. "Steel weakens me," he said in a hissed breath.

Well, well, well, hiding in my truck *had* been the right move. I tried to conceal my smirk, then jerked my chin in the direction of the teeth. "It kind of sucks that you didn't get any more trophies this time around," I needled.

He touched the teeth strung together and weaved into his long, dark hair. "You humans have increased in population, have spread out to take more of my land. It is hard to retrieve a trophy when the threat of discovery is unavoidable." He tilted his head to the side—listening.

Then I heard it.

"Cat!" Sawyer called frantically as he returned to me.

I felt his fear like it was my own. It tightened my chest. Made my breath saw through my lungs.

The Amaroq smiled nefariously. In that moment, I saw what he was going to do.

"Sawyer!" I yelled in warning. "Run!"

"Anansi," the Amaroq commanded at the same time. "Kill him."

The spider scuttled past us, the gold slave band flashing as she moved.

Sawyer pulled out his Glock and took aim, but he wasn't fast enough. Anansi struck.

"Sawyer!" I tried to run to him, but my feet were suddenly— inexplicably—rooted to the spot.

"Stay and watch the show," the Amaroq cooed, amused.

"Let me go," I ground out, trying to move my feet. No, not my feet. They *could* move—it was the soles of my boots that couldn't because thousands of spiders had woven a multitude of silk over them. Leaning down, I tore down the zippers on the sides. I felt like I'd stepped into a chest freezer as soon as the soles of my feet made contact with the cave floor.

With Reaver in hand, I ran toward the giant spider, wondering how in the hell I was going to find my partner in there. I called his name again, desperately searching for a way to get to him.

"Pussy cat," Sawyer called, his voice clear and calm. "I'm okay."

I scanned the frame of limbs covering him. "Where are you?" I yelled, desperately searching for him.

I can't resist his orders much longer, Anansi whispered frantically into my head. *Free me!*

Free her?

... *Free her.*

... *Free her.*

That's what the dryad had told me.

I stared at Anansi.

Is this who I was supposed to help? Not Rachel?

Scanning her body, I caught a flash of gold from...

... the slave band!

I lifted the sword to the gilt fetter and touched the steel against it. Reaver hummed as it tasted an ancient power, my opal flaring to life too.

"No!" the Amaroq bellowed behind me.

With my free hand, I pulled out my Glock and took aim at his heart. "One more step, wolf-boy, and I'll make sure to stuff you and mount you in my living room."

His eyes flashed savage red as he bared his teeth—his much-too-large-for-his-mouth teeth. His jaw popped, hinging open like a snake's to house his new grill. Keeping my gun trained on him, I risked a glance at Reaver to see how it was progressing. The gold was melting away under the touch of the sword, changing color from yellow gold to molten red as it dripped onto the cave floor. The heat that beaded off it was fierce, but Anansi showed no indication she was in pain.

I turned my attention back to the Amaroq when there was a snarl that set the fine hairs on the back of my neck on end. He had changed into his wolf form. At least as tall as a thoroughbred, just as Rachel had said, he stalked toward me with shaggy black fur and fangs the size of my index finger flashing in his huge mouth. Along his spine, jagged quills protruded from his back, bristling like an agitated porcupine's. He growled, making the blood in my veins freeze, my muscles lock down tight on my bones.

That was all the warning I got.

He launched himself at me.

I squeezed the trigger, firing three shots into his body.

Bang!

Bang!

Bang!

They didn't even slow him.

"Dammit!"

Diving out of the way, I landed hard on my stomach and shoulder, my temple making contact with a loose stone about the size of a baseball. Man, that was going to leave a bruise. Blood spilled from the new laceration, dribbling down my forehead. I rolled over onto my back, aiming my Glock at him in a two-handed grip. The slave band *clunked* to the cold stone floor, and the accompanying ripple of power slammed into me.

There was a flash of bright light, and when it disappeared, a beautiful African woman stood where the spider had been. Her head was swathed in a striped scarf in earthy tones of ochres, greens and golds. Her eyes were the color of milk—a stark contrast to the richness of her skin.

Along the arches of her cheekbones, brows, and chin, white scar tissue formed a geometric pattern. Two different bands wrapped around her biceps, but unlike the slave band, these were filled with the same shapes as the scars on her face. There were bracelets around her wrists too—smaller this time, but the same pattern was repeated.

A full skirt and bustier top clad her slender body—the whole ensemble finished off by a thick beaded necklace made of the same colors as her headwrap.

The Amaroq backed away a step.

I was suddenly pressed back into the ground, Sawyer's panic threading through me.

"Don't look in her eyes," he whispered in a harsh breath.

"Why not?"

There was a savage snarl. I turned back in time to see the Amaroq leap at Anansi. With a wry grin on her full lips, she did nothing but watch him. I tried to shove Sawyer off me.

"We have to help her," I hissed at him, lumbering to my feet.

There was a dull *thud* that made me look again.

I stared for a moment, trying to figure out if I was seeing things correctly. The Amaroq was lying on his side, frozen in his attacking position. Anansi walked up to the petrified Amaroq and crouched beside him. That smile of hers was still in place.

From the corner of my eye, I saw thousands of spiders emerge from wherever they were hiding, crawling along the walls and venturing onto the stone floor. Anansi lowered a hand, some of the spiders crawling onto her palm. One particularly large one about the size of my hand scuttled up her torso and perched on her shoulder like it was a beloved parrot.

I shuddered, keeping an eye on the spiders inching closer to us.

She looked over then and stood, her full skirts swaying as she approached. Every single muscle in my body tensed, and I stared hard at the stone floor beneath my feet.

"You have nothing to fear from me, Cat McKenzie," she said in a smooth, slightly accented voice. Reaching up, she placed her finger under my chin and forced my head up. I kept my eyes firmly shut just in case.

"You have nothing to fear from me," she repeated. "Open your eyes."

I cracked one eye, then the other, blinking at the otherworldly woman in front of me. "Please don't petrify me," I blurted out.

Anansi chuckled. "I owe you a debt of thanks." She glanced over at the petrified Amaroq then back at me. "You have released me from over three centuries of enslavement. I cannot begin to tell you what it feels like to have my freedom back."

"Three *centuries*? You've been a slave for *three centuries*?"

"Yes. I came over from Africa in the 18th century looking for an adventure. Life had begun to bore me, and being the goddess I am, I thought myself indestructible. After all, I can change into a spider at will." She smiled, but there was no humor in it. "I'd heard the American colony enjoyed the use of slaves, so I avoided them, heading into your modern-day Alaska. Only another slave master found me—one much more long-lived than a human."

"How did he capture you?"

She shrugged her slender shoulders, reminding me of the spider that rested there. She stroked the abdomen on the arachnid then let out a small sigh. "Men have always wanted power—ever since the beginning of time. It's in their nature to seek it, and the Amaroq used mine to his advantage. He knew who I was the moment he saw me. Being a Shaman himself, he saw me coming and began fashioning a slave band. Caught unaware, he secured it around my waist and commanded me into my spider form to protect him while he slept. He also knew to blindfold me so I could not petrify him."

The reminder of her ability made me shuffle back a step.

Anansi laughed. "Worry not, Cat McKenzie. I choose who I petrify. The Amaroq thought it was involuntary, which was why he took the precaution of the blindfold. He commanded I not remove it in his presence, and I was compelled to follow the decree."

I frowned at her statement. "If it was voluntary, why did you petrify that construction worker?"

Darkness bled into her white eyes. "I was charged to kill the man, but I resisted the order as best I could. At least petrified, he would not have to suffer like he would have if the Amaroq had mauled him. What I did was a mercy."

Except that the wood sprites had made him their personal all-you-can-eat buffet. Although, if I had to choose between being terrified to death and ripped to shreds by a wolf, I would've chosen the easier route too.

"So, what now? Are you going to return to Africa?"

Anansi thought about that for a moment, a small grin playing on her lips. Raising her hand to her shoulder, the spider there climbed onto her palm. The goddess stared at it with love in her eyes. "Perhaps I'll stay here for a while longer, then see where fate takes me. Goodbye, Cat. I owe you a debt of gratitude. If ever you need help, my spiders will aid you. Just ask them."

The spider in her palm lowered its body into what I could've sworn was a bow. I blinked, swallowing back the urge to scream.

"Th-th-thank you."

With a small incline of her head, she called, "Come my darlings," to the spiders and wandered farther into the darkest part of the cave. I stood completely still as a sea of spiders rushed to follow their master, the sound of their legs moving along the stone, something that would haunt me for the rest of my life.

I yelped when I felt a hand on my lower back, then sagged in relief when I realized it was Sawyer. His chocolate and whisky scent wrapped around me like a tangible caress.

"Spiders still freak me out," I said then looked at the Amaroq. "What are we going to do with him?"

Sawyer stepped a little closer and inspected the petrified form. "I don't know. We can't arrest him. As far as I know, once someone is petrified, there's only one way to reverse it."

"How?"

"Anansi would have to do it."

I snorted. "Good luck getting her on board with that." I stared at the wolf, remembering my words to him. "Can we take him home?"

Sawyer's brows rose. "Run that by me again."

"Home. Can we take him home? I promised to stuff and mount him, but taxidermy always makes me feel *ick*. This way, I'll have a clear conscious because he's… you know, *not* technically dead."

Sawyer shook his head.

"Come on. Think of it as my New Year's present."

"Gifts aren't typically exchanged at New Year," he deadpanned.

"Oh, Sawyer, you have so much to learn about me." I patted his cheek. "Any holiday is cause to give me presents. Preferably unicorn-related ones."

"Noted," he said with a wry smile. He turned his attention back to the Amaroq and sighed. "How are we supposed to get it home?"

I clapped him on the shoulder. "I'll leave the logistics to you."

20

"**I**s that what I think it is?" I asked Sawyer as we pulled into the parking lot at the precinct the next day. A few bays over, there were three black Ford Crown Vics circa 1993. Sliding off the back of Sawyer's Ducati, I took off my helmet and studied the nondescript early model cars that were quintessentially 'cop.'

Sawyer joined me a moment later. "You know what, they just might be."

I pumped my fist into the air.

PIG *finally* had their own cars.

No more destruction of *my* property.

Suck it, supes.

"When can I drive one?" I asked, excitement bubbling through me.

"Let's just go and check in with Vaile first."

Sawyer and I headed inside, walking the gauntlet down to our offices in the back. Smith stepped into my path about halfway along. He eyed me like I was worse than the shit on his shoe, then Sawyer.

"I see your department finally got what they've been begging for," he said in a sneer.

"Nah, otherwise you'd be forced to dress in a diaper every day," I shot back with a sweet butter-wouldn't-melt-in-my-mouth smile.

He ground his teeth together audibly. "I meant the UC cars."

I grinned even more widely at him, his sour mood doing nothing to dampen my excitement over finally having our own cars. "Oh, yeah, you saw them, did you?"

"It's kind of hard to miss those pieces of junk out the front."

Waggling my finger in his face, I sing-songed, "Someone's sounding jealous. Want to come and join PIG just so you can ride around in one? I'll even let you call shotgun."

"Take your finger out of my face, McKenzie," he growled, grabbing my wrist. The moment he made contact with me, Sawyer was there. Balling up Smith's shirt in his hand, he yanked the guy off his feet and slammed him against the closest wall.

The rest of the occupants of the bullpen stopped whatever they were doing, looks of shock on their face.

"Disrespect my partner again, Smith, and I'll be forced to remove your intestines through your mouth. *Touch* my partner again, and you don't want to know how much I'll enjoy destroying you."

He let Smith go, throwing him to one side like he was yesterday's garbage. The POS landed on someone's desk, breaking the piece of furniture in two. Shards of wood and paper flew into the air, showering Smith and anyone within a couple of feet of him.

"Are you okay?" Sawyer asked me, his gray eyes dark with rage instead of lust this time—at least I thought it was rage. Seeing him show everyone just how strong he was nearly made my ovaries explode.

"Fine." I drew him away. "And if we didn't have to be here right now," I added, lowering my voice. "I'd totally drag you into the supply closet and have my way with you."

"Did that turn you on, pussy cat?'" he asked, his voice husky—tempting.

"I'm sure you know it did." Although, why it did I wasn't so sure. "Come on. We have to speak to Wolfe, and we're running late."

A few steps down the hallway, Sawyer knocked on Wolfe's door.

"Enter!" our boss barked.

We walked inside and found him behind his desk, his forearms on the blotter, his hands clasped together in front of him. "Where are we on the Forest Lodge case?"

Sawyer glanced at me and nodded.

"Case closed," I replied.

Wolfe's brows rose to his hairline. "Run that by me again."

"We got it. The full confession, blah, blah, blah."

"Blah, blah, blah? I hope that's not going to be in your report."

"I'll pretty up the language, but the bad guy has been caught, the young girl has been rescued, and people won't be getting killed up in the mountains again."

Our boss nodded. "How'd it go down?"

"Big fight. I won, naturally."

He eyed the cut on my temple and the surrounding bruise on my face. "Naturally. Was the Amaroq arrested?"

Sawyer and I shared a look.

"He was… detained," I hedged. Because you couldn't lie to Wolfe. His werewolf senses could detect it.

"He was petrified by Anansi, who he was keeping his prisoner to protect him while he slept."

"Anansi," Vaile repeated. "The goddess?"

"Who turns into a spider," I supplied helpfully.

He leaned back in his chair. "She was cursed by a sangoma, a shaman, to take the form of a spider after she tricked the sangoma's wife into giving her their firstborn son in exchange for protection."

I was impressed. I had to get started on that compendium. "How do you know this?"

"I read, Officer McKenzie."

Ooo, was it a little frosty in here?

"Where is Anansi now?" he asked, looking at Sawyer. "Will she be any more trouble?"

Sawyer said, "She disappeared into the cave system. All she wanted was her freedom, so I doubt she'll be bothering anyone soon."

He studied them for a moment more. "You saw the new UC cars outside?"

"Yes, sir."

"You and McKenzie will get one."

"And the others?"

"Brax will be taking a more active role in the unit and will partner with one. Ben will take another." He let out a sigh, rubbing his eyes with his thumb and forefinger. "Losing Hayliel was a blow to the unit we didn't need." He stared at us for a moment. "Are you still planning on having a New Year's party?"

"Yes?" I replied, already knowing what he was going to ask.

"Make sure to invite the recruits. Use it as a bonding experience."

As we left his office, I stage whispered, "We're not actually going to do that, are we?"

"Why not?"

Why not? I didn't need weird new people messing up my apartment vibes. I didn't say that, of course. Instead, I shrugged. "Just curious. Wolfe can't actually *order* us to invite them, though, right?"

"Think of it as a getting-to-know-you exercise."

"I always hated them in school."

"I'll let you tell Wolfe that you don't want to play nice with the new recruits then."

21

"Hey, this is a great specimen," Brad said, studying the leaping form of the Amaroq that I'd had Sawyer display in our living room. Was it morbid to have a murdering Inuit legend on display like real taxidermy in our apartment?

Maybe.

Probably.

I did warn him.

"You spliced it with a porcupine though, right?" He indicated the quills along the Amaroq's spine. "Fascinating. I have a collection of taxidermy at my family's lodge," Brad added, oblivious to my own inner dialogue. "We don't have a wolf though... and nothing this big in a full-body mount. It's extraordinary."

He touched the Amaroq's flank, and my opal pulsed with heat beneath my sweater. Brad shook his hand out like he'd just received an electric shock then looked up at the ceiling, then at the ground around the Amaroq's feet.

"What are you looking for, baby?" Sasha asked, taking a sip from her champagne flute.

"It's cold."

"It's petrified," I told him, smiling benignly.

"Petrified?" Sasha asked, her eyes darting to the Amaroq. "What do you mean?"

"I mean, he's not stuffed and mounted." I jabbed my finger at the wolf. "That's the Amaroq—an Inuit legend, FYI—in his wolf form, who was petrified by an African goddess spider shifter who I set free from his enslavement."

Both of them stared at me, their mouths slightly hanging open.

"What? Too much truth?"

My best friend edged away from the wolf like it was going to suddenly un-petrify and attack her. Brad—to his credit—simply looked amused.

"You said she was funny," he joked with Sasha. If he wanted to think I was joking, that was fine by me. "Not sure about the sex doll perched on his tail, though."

"Neither was I," Sawyer said, crossing the room and handing a bottle of beer to Brad. "If you haven't figured it out yet, Cat has a warped sense of humor. She was joking, of course, about the petrified wolf. It's just been stuffed and mounted."

I shot him a look. Like hell I was joking. I folded my arms over my chest, irritated. Sawyer placed his hand on the small of my back and whispered into my ear, "You're scaring the humans. Why don't you go and talk to one of the new recruits?"

"Do I have to?"

"You're the host of this party, so yeah."

Grumbling but knowing he was right, I walked to where Pyro was standing in the corner. His dark hair was shaggy around his face, the tips dancing with flames. Unlike when he was in the office, they were small—barely there—and I wondered whether the size of those flames had a direct link to his emotions.

"Hey," I said. "I'm Cat."

His golden eyes were reproachful. "I know," he replied, staring straight ahead. "Human." His tone was arsenic-laced—derisive.

I crossed my arms. "You don't have to say it like that."

Narrowing his eyes, he demanded, "Like what?"

"Like I'm a parasite or something."

He bared his teeth in the parody of a grin, steam curling out from between his lips.

I pointed at his mouth. "You've got a little something in your teeth."

"Yeah. It's called the raging inferno of my anger and disdain for all of humanity."

"Wow. I thought Ben was disgruntled. And just like Ben, I bet all this cynical snarliness is a front, right? Deep down, you're a teddy bear who enjoys the witty humor of a human colleague."

He gave me a flat stare, the flames in his hair growing in intensity. *Totally called it.*

"Look, can you take the bonfire outside? You'll set off my smoke alarms." I patted him on the shoulder, then sucked in a hiss. I looked at my fingertips—they were charred like I'd just brushed against a cold fireplace, but they burned like I'd touched an open flame. I blinked at him. "What are you?"

"Bored." Unfolding his arms, he stalked away. I glanced down to see there were faint scorch marks on the hardwood.

"Don't take his disdain for you personally," someone said behind me. I half-turned my head to find Jacob standing near the wall, his arms casually folded over his chest. His black wings were obnoxiously flared, showing off the fine ribbons of iridescent shine threaded through them. Like his wings, his skin looked like it had been slathered in diamond dust, the sheen matching his silver hair. "But if you're looking for a friend, I volunteer."

"As tribute, I hope. I wonder how quickly you'd get killed in an engineered dystopian gladiatorial-style battle?" I tapped my chin in thought.

"*The Hunger Games*," he replied. "I love that movie."

Finally! A supe who got pop culture references. Too bad he was a douche-canoe. "What do you want, Jacob?"

"Wolfe told us to get to know each other, and it's *you* I want to get to know the most."

"Why?"

He took a lock of my hair in between his fingers. "Are you kidding me? You're gorgeous."

Taking a step back, I severed the contact. "As much as I'd enjoy seeing Sawyer make your skull into his own personal urinal for touching me, I—"

"So, it's true then? You and Sawyer are a thing?"

"Would it make a difference if we were?"

He gave me a cavalier smile. "Of course."

Somehow, I didn't believe him. There was just something about him that set the hairs on the back of my neck on end. "What kind of supe are you?"

He flared his wings pretentiously, shaking them out. "An angel."

I canted my head to the side. Surely if he were an angel, I'd feel something other than distrust. "Highly doubtful. What are you *really*?"

He shrugged, all *hey-shucks-it-was-worth-a-try*. "False angel."

"I am supposed to know what that means?"

"My kind is generally known to be untrustworthy, lying, cheating bastards."

Ah. "And you joined the cops? That doesn't seem like something an untrustworthy, lying, cheating bastard would do. Your words, not mine."

Flashing me a grin, he leaned one shoulder against the wall, turning his body in my direction, and folding his wings away. The tips Swiffered the floor nicely. I'd have to get him to do the whole apartment. "I don't believe in stereotyping, do you?"

I didn't know. It had kind of worked in my favor before. "What kind of supe is Pyro?"

One of his brows winged up in question. "What will you trade for that information?"

Trade? "Ah, nothing?"

"You don't just expect me to answer your questions for free, do you?" When I opened my mouth then closed it again, he added, "False angels trade information, not give it away for free. I've already given you one free answer. So, what do you have to trade?"

"I thought false angels were also untrustworthy. How can I believe a word you'll say?"

His returning grin was tight. "And you've caught me. All right, I just wanted to see what you'd give me."

I scowled. "You didn't have a lot of friends growing up, did you?"

Although he shrugged like he didn't give a damn, I thought I saw a glimmer of pain there. "Pyro is a Phoenix Shifter."

Ah, that would explain the flames then. "And what does that mean, exactly?"

He smiled at me again and shrugged one shoulder. "I think it'll be fun to watch you find that out on your own."

And with that, he sauntered away, joining Brax and his mate, Andrea, in the kitchen.

"See, that wasn't so hard, was it?" Sawyer asked, coming to join me. "Although, I would like to know what you told Jacob to stop him from touching you."

"You saw that?"

He nodded stiffly. "Yeah, and I've got to tell you, all I want to do now is stake my claim on you so he never attempts it again."

I patted him on the cheek. "You're cute when you're jealous."

He playfully nipped at my fingers. "So, what did you say to him?"

I shrugged and said, "I told him you'd use his skull as a urinal if he touched me again."

He laughed—the dark, rich sound like a physical caress on every single one of my erogenous zones. I gasped, waves of desire crashing through me. Catching the scent of my lust, Sawyer stepped a little closer, pressing himself against me.

"I can have everyone out of here in under thirty seconds," he growled. "Just give me the word."

Holy. Shit. I licked my lips. "Tempting. *So* tempting, but—" I stopped when Kayla, the coffee-filching harpy, re-entered the living room wearing one of my unicorn t-shirts. "What the hell does she think she's doing?" I demanded, taking a step away.

Sawyer followed my line of sight and quickly grabbed my wrist, pulling me to a stop. "Easy there, pussy cat."

Turning to glare at him, I sputtered, "She can't just... *steal* my stuff and wear it!"

"Yes, I can," Kayla replied from across the room, buffing her long red nails on *my* shirt. "I'm a harpy with far superior strength and cunning."

"You're also a guest in my apartment," I ground out.

Her multi-hued eyes glimmered with amusement. "And as a guest, I should get dibs on whatever I like." Pulling at the bottom of the shirt, she added, "And I like this right now."

"Kayla, are you stirring the pot over there?" Jacob called. The arrogant asshole had his wings out on full display again like the giant tool that he was.

"Stirring." The harpy shrugged. "Adding more spice. Take your pick."

"I don't like her," I told Sawyer before stalking away to scan the corners of the ceiling.

"What are you doing now?" he asked behind me.

"Looking for any spiders I can sic on her. And, hey," I pointed at the pristine square-set ceiling. "Not so much as a cobweb floating around up there. You're cleaning too thoroughly."

He quirked up a brow. "You're going to complain about my cleaning?"

Sasha emerged from the hallway, smoothing her hands down the front of her jeans. She scanned the room, smiling when she caught sight of me.

"Oh, look, there's Brad. Why don't you go and speak to him so I can have some private time with my girl?" I shoved Sawyer in the back in the direction of Sasha's fiancé. Bewildered, he walked toward the other guy.

"So, I have to know," my friend said to me. "Why did you invite all these supes to your New Year's party?"

I groaned. "I didn't. Well, some of them I did. Ben the Wendigo and Brax, the werewolf and his mate, were invited. The Three Shit-Bag-Ateers are here because my boss ordered Sawyer and me to *bond* with them."

"Who are they?"

"New PIG recruits."

"You're joking, right?"

"Afraid not. We'll have one of them shadowing us for the next little while, so they get used to things."

She stared at them all, her gaze lingering on Jacob for a moment longer than the others. Then, she frowned and pointed at Kayla. "Isn't that your shirt?"

"Yeah. She's a harpy. Apparently, a kleptomaniac as well."

She nodded. "I noticed her proclivity for the five-finger discount. I saw her lifting a guy's wallet right out of his pocket."

Annnd sure enough, Kayla was brandishing her spoils at me—Ben's wallet—wearing a huge smile that seemed to say *Just try and stop me.*

"Yeah, well, she'd better watch herself. Ben is into human flesh, but I'm sure harpy would be close enough." I dragged my gaze off the thieving harpy. "Anyway, how's the wedding planning? Did you see any dresses you liked?"

"No, not yet. I was waiting until you were free again to come with me."

"How about tomorrow? Unless something gruesome is called in, I'm all yours."

"That just sounds like you're tempting fate."

I lifted a shoulder in a shrug. "Maybe—"

"Hey!" Ben suddenly roared. I spun around to find him with his hand wrapped around Kayla's wrist, his cell phone trapped between her sticky fingers. "That's mine, harpy."

"I found it on the ground," Kayla replied, confident.

Yanking her off balance, Ben pulled her closer to his face—his human mask beginning to flicker with his growing annoyance. It revealed the deer skull and horns that lay beneath. When they were nose-to-nose, Ben said something too softly for me to hear, but Kayla's face drained of color.

"All right, let's break it up," Jacob said, arrogantly walking to the pair and pulling Kayla away. To the harpy, he said, "Give him back his phone."

"But I found it," she replied, sullen.

"In my pocket," Ben spit out, glaring at the brown-haired beauty. He patted down his other pocket and growled. Holding out his hand, he flexed his fingers. "Give it *and my wallet* to me now, or I'll cut off both of your hands."

She handed both items over. "Oh, please, I'll regrow them in a week."

Ben shoved his finger in her face. "Long enough for you to be in complete agony as you starved. From now on, stay out of my way."

"Whoa, what do you think you're doing there, my man?" Jacob asked, stepping between them once more.

Ben turned his ire to the other male. "And you stay out of my face too. I know what you are *Nephilim*." He spat the last word like it was diseased.

Nephilim? Was that another name for a false angel?

The wendigo stalked toward me, and I spun around, hoping he hadn't seen me.

"Did he see me?" I asked Sasha from the corner of my mouth.

"Yes," she whispered back.

"McKenzie, I'm going," Ben said, his voice warping with his rage.

I turned around, saying too brightly, "Oh, hey, I didn't see you there."

He gave me a flat look, and I swallowed hard.

Gruffly, *begrudgingly*, he said, "Happy new year. I guess."

"Happy new year—" I called after him, my words cut off by the slamming of the front door.

"This party sucks," Kayla called out. "What we need is music. I want to dance." She tugged at Pyro's hand, but he remained in place, watching her with his golden eyes and flaming hair.

"Baby?" Brad said to Sasha, handing over her jacket. "I think we should probably go. We have to make an appearance at my client's party, too."

"I forgot about that," she replied, then look at me apologetically.

"It's okay. You guys can go. I only wanted to check out Brad for myself." I pulled her in for a hug. "Enjoy the rest of your night."

"You too. Try not to let the harpy ruin it for you."

I glanced over my shoulder to find the harpy in question slamming back tequila shots then tearing off her shirt—*my* shirt—to reveal one of *my* bras.

"I'm going to kill her," I muttered under my breath.

"Remember, you hate getting blood on the carpet!" Sasha called out as she and Brad left the apartment.

Marching over to Kayla, I yanked the bottle of tequila from her hand. "I want you gone."

She gave the picture-perfect pout. "I'm not finished partying yet."

"Yeah, you are."

"Come on, Cat," Jacob started.

Rounding on him, I snarled, "Shut it. You're going too."

"Only if it's with you to your bedroom."

I glared at him. "Seriously? Get the fuck out of here."

Two down.

One to go.

I looked at Pyro, who was already getting his jacket and making his way to the door.

"I guess we'll go too then?" Brax offered.

"Sorry," I told him. "I didn't realize I'd get this ticked off so quickly."

His mate, Andrea, gave me a hug. "Harpies can be a handful," was all she said, sliding her arms into her jacket.

When everyone was gone, Sawyer hugged me from behind, resting his chin on the top of my head. "That escalated quickly."

"At least I didn't get the trident out."

There was a long pause. "You have a trident?"

I spun around. "I've said it before, and I'll say it again… pop culture is lost on supes."

Shaking his head, he flashed me a devilish smile. "Well, now that we're alone…" he began in a seductive purr, "… we can pick up where we left off before you started yelling at Kayla."

"She deserved to be yelled at."

Pinching my chin between his thumb and forefinger, he tilted my face up to meet his—efficiently shutting me up. I got lost in the darkening depths of his gray eyes, a lightning storm sweeping across the horizon. Desire for my consort hit me with all the finesse of a wrecking ball, the strength of feelings leaving my knees weak and my head fuzzy.

As if sensing this, he swooped an arm under my knees and hefted me into his arms. Wrapping mine around his neck, our lips came together in a violent, erotic clash. The stubble on his cheeks and chin abrading my skin deliciously.

"Ready to ring in the new year with me… in bed?" he asked raggedly when we finally broke apart, pressing our foreheads together until we were breathing each other's air.

Yeah, I was. I was *so* ready.

As we left the living room, I blew the Amaroq a kiss then killed the lights with the toe of my shoe as we passed the switch.

"Do you think it went really badly?" I asked, playing with the hair at the nape of his neck.

Sawyer chucked, pushing into his dark bedroom. "It could've been better. I'll just blame your grouchy mood on a lack of orgasms. Something I'm hoping to change in the very near future." He hit the lights, and a small gasp escaped me.

His bedroom had changed. Gone were the dark gray sheets and comforter. Now, the bed was covered in my unicorn bedspread—the one that was supposed to be in my room. Wiggling from his grasp, I took it all in. The two armchairs and couch were still there, but they now had unicorn throw pillows adorning their cushions. A soft-looking unicorn blanket was folded over the back of the couch. But the unicorn goodness didn't stop there.

Sawyer had moved five more display cases into the corner, some of my new pieces in the collection on the shelves. I walked up to the glass, pressing my nose against it as I peered inside.

"Do you like it?" he asked behind me.

I spun to face him. "Like? Try *love*, but..." I frowned. "Why?"

"You said you wanted a present for New Year's—something unicorn related—so this is your gift."

"Buuut shouldn't this stuff be in *my* room, then?"

Moving slowly, he anchored his hands on my waist and stared intensely into my eyes. "I want you to move in."

I laughed. "We already did that."

He shook his head. "What I mean is, I want you to move into my room. With me." He gestured to the redecorated space. "I want you with all your crazy unicorn paraphernalia. Your warped sense of humor. Your caffeine addiction. I want you in my bed every night and there every morning. I want you, Cat." His gaze darted away briefly before returning to my face, indecision playing in his eyes. Clearing his throat, he whispered, "I love you."

World.

Rocked.

"I-I… I don't know what to say." The L-bomb had been dropped, and I hadn't taken cover. I was bathing in the fallout. He *loved* me.

Before I could say anything, Sawyer added, "Move in with me properly, pussy cat."

I looked around at the unicorn pretties then turned to the man who had changed his personal space into somewhere I could share with him.

"Okay, Sawyer. I'll move in with you."

His happiness eclipsed the room as he lifted and spun me around. When my feet touched the floor once more, he kissed me, his tongue sweeping into my mouth in a long, lingering kiss. The kiss became an inferno of lust between us, scorching me wherever I touched him.

Even though it took all my strength, I pulled away, glad to find him panting just as I was. "You mentioned something about orgasms?"

With the sexiest growl I'd ever heard, he picked me up and threw me onto the bed. Before I could even bounce, he was on me, pressing his huge erection into the apex of my thighs. I groaned, throwing my head back. Sawyer bit the cords of my neck, laving away the sting with his wicked tongue.

In a sex-roughed voice, he told me, "Yeah, I did. Let's get started." Kiss. "Right." A slide of his hand between my thighs. "Now."

BAD WOLF

A CAT MCKENZIE NOVEL

www.ingramcontent.com/pod-product-compliance
Lightning Source LLC
Chambersburg PA
CBHW050929120626
46552CB00001B/114